KT-119-605

WHITE LACE

Dismissed from her employment at the academy, the future seems bleak for Barbara Thorpe. But a whirlwind romance leads to marriage when she meets Kieran Alexander. However, upon being taken to his home, Rowan Castle, she is overawed by its grandness. Barbara is further disquieted by the fact that she knows nothing about him, and by meeting the beautiful but arrogant Kerensa Templeton. First her marriage, then her life, will be threatened before she can discover both the truth and real happiness . . .

Books by Rosemary A. Smith
in the Linford Romance Library:

THE AMETHYST BROOCH
THE BLUEBELL WOOD
THE BROODING LAKE
A STRANGER'S KISS

SPECIAL MESSAGE TO READERS

This book is published under the auspices of

THE ULVERSCROFT FOUNDATION

(registered charity No. 264873 UK)

Established in 1972 to provide funds for research, diagnosis and treatment of eye diseases. Examples of contributions made are: —

A Children's Assessment Unit at Moorfield's Hospital, London.

•

Twin operating theatres at the Western Ophthalmic Hospital, London.

•

A Chair of Ophthalmology at the Royal Australian College of Ophthalmologists.

•

The Ulverscroft Children's Eye Unit at the Great Ormond Street Hospital For Sick Children, London.

You can help further the work of the Foundation by making a donation or leaving a legacy. Every contribution, no matter how small, is received with gratitude. Please write for details to:

**THE ULVERSCROFT FOUNDATION,
The Green, Bradgate Road, Anstey,
Leicester LE7 7FU, England.
Telephone: (0116) 236 4325**

**In Australia write to:
THE ULVERSCROFT FOUNDATION,
c/o The Royal Australian and New Zealand
College of Ophthalmologists,
94-98 Chalmers Street, Surry Hills,
N.S.W. 2010, Australia**

ROSEMARY A. SMITH

WHITE LACE

Complete and Unabridged

LINFORD
Leicester

First published in Great Britain in 2007

First Linford Edition
published 2008

Copyright © 2007 by Rosemary A. Smith
All rights reserved

British Library CIP Data

Smith, Rosemary A.
    White lace.—Large print ed.—
Linford romance library
1. Love stories
2. Large type books
I. Title
823.9′2 [F]

ISBN 978–1–84782–225–3

20180352

MORAY COUNCIL

DEPARTMENT OF TECHNICAL

& LEISURE SERVICES

F

Published by
F. A. Thorpe (Publishing)
Anstey, Leicestershire

Set by Words & Graphics Ltd.
Anstey, Leicestershire
Printed and bound in Great Britain by
T. J. International Ltd., Padstow, Cornwall

This book is printed on acid-free paper

For my two lovely sisters
Irene and Ruth — Friends Forever

Acknowledgements

With thanks to my cousin Barbara Newns of Shrewsbury for giving me the inspiration for my story 'White Lace' at Claire and Glen's wedding.

My grateful thanks to George Gingell of Budleigh Salterton, a connoisseur of music boxes, for the wonderful morning I spent in his home, and for all the valued advice he gave me for my story 'A Stranger's Kiss'.

1

I first met Kieran Alexander on an autumn day in Shrewsbury in 1883. I'd been looking out of the long glass window of the library at the scene below. I could see Shrewsbury Castle opposite me. Its red walls mellowed to a warm orange by the early afternoon sun matching the autumn leaves which covered the ground on this late September afternoon.

I had little to look forward to, no family and no friends except for Clarissa who taught at the Academy as I had done until two weeks ago, when I was dismissed for taking a pupil's side, when to my mind she had been treated unfairly. What path lay before me now I had no idea, a post as a governess perhaps, but with no recommendation I doubted whether this would be possible. So I spent my days in the warmth of the library reading books about Elizabeth 1 and the Tudors, a subject I was avid about.

It filled my days and then the evenings were spent alone in my dingy room except for an hour or two which Clarissa managed to share with me. Thankfully I was surviving on savings I'd accumulated while working and living in at the Academy.

A footstep on the dark polished floor behind me interrupted my thoughts and I turned to see who other than myself wished to use the reference department. A silent exclamation escaped my lips as I looked at the tall handsome fair-haired man who stood before me by one of the many tables.

His piercing blue eyes met my grey ones across the room and my heart thudded in my chest, so much so that I was afraid the gentleman would hear it.

'Good afternoon, Miss . . . ?' he queried in a soft masculine voice. I had an instant attraction to him as if someone had dealt me a harsh blow.

My legs were weak and trembling and I prayed my voice would not betray my overwhelming emotion.

'Miss Thorpe, Barbara Thorpe.' I answered. 'And you, Sir, are?'

'Kieran Alexander.' As he spoke he stepped nearer towards me, I noted the grey bowler hat he held under one arm and the immaculate grey single-breasted morning coat which he wore, together with a white high-necked shirt and red necktie. He looked so handsome and perfect, I could not draw my eyes away, although propriety urged me to do so.

He drew towards me and whispered, 'We cannot talk here or the librarian will admonish us.' He said looking across at the prim grey-haired woman who sat at her desk watching us.

I laughed quietly for his eyes were full of mischief and gaiety.

'So Miss Thorpe, will you do me the honour of joining me for afternoon tea?' I could not say no, no matter how much my head said beware, you don't

3

know this man, my heart screamed, yes!

'Yes,' I agreed picking up my reticule from the table. I suddenly felt drab in my brown dress and jacket with my best beige-decorated bonnet, but my face must have held a look of eagerness and pleasure and I felt an emotion I had not felt before, it crept over my whole being uninvited yet welcomed and I had yet to work out what it was.

From that day we spent most of our days together. We walked around the castle and spent much time in all weathers walking by the River Severn. We dined each evening at the Clarence Hotel where Kieran was staying.

On each occasion I'd worn my best beige poplin gown and stitched on various collars and cuffs and added trimmings to alter the gown's appearance. How I wished I could buy another gown, but Kieran was happy as I was, so it mattered little.

I told him my life story, but he told me little about himself, except that he lived in a castle in North Wales with his brother and sister. Sometimes Kieran's face held a faraway look, but he was soon smiling again. There was a lot I wanted to ask him, for one thing why he didn't go home, but something stopped me. Was it a premonition that if I asked him all this would end? And the Lord knew how much I didn't want this ever to be over, this dream world that we were living in, so enrapt was I in the moment that I didn't give the future a thought. How I was to wish one day that I had.

We were dining on the evening of Christmas day at the hotel, red candles were lit all around us giving everything including Kieran and myself a warm rosy glow. I was partaking of my Christmas pudding and Kieran was watching me, a serious expression on his face. My heart started beating faster with an irrational fear.

'I have to return home,' he had said quietly and my heart sank, tears pricked at my eyes and I pushed the plate which held the pudding away from me and dabbed at my mouth with the red napkin.

'Soon?' was all I could say. My eyes cast down not daring to look at him for fear he would see the tears.

'I want you to come with me Barbara, as my wife.' His words were so unexpected I looked directly at him and mumbled.

'Your wife? But surely you would wish to marry with your family around you.'

'No.' He had said adamantly, 'I wish to marry in January, quietly without any fuss. You know I was attracted to you from the moment I set eyes on you. I just want it to be us and a couple of witnesses. Please say yes.' So saying he took my hand across the table and squeezed it gently.

'Yes,' I whispered, 'yes I will marry you. Wherever and whenever you want.' I agreed without further questioning.

'Splendid!' Kieran had replied. 'I will make the arrangements.'

On Boxing Day Clarissa came to

spend the day with me. I danced around my drab dreary room with joy in my heart as I related to my friend my good fortune.

'But you hardly know him,' Clarissa had said, and still no doubt entered my mind. All that mattered to me what that I became Mrs Kieran Alexander, Kieran's wife.

The day of our wedding arrived, Clarissa was to be one of our witnesses as was Mrs Malvers, an acquaintance of Kieran's, who was staying at the same hotel as he. A carriage had been sent for Clarissa and I and on my arrival at the chapel Kieran had placed my arm through his and smiled down at me encouragingly with Clarissa and Mrs Malvers behind us.

The interior of the small stone chapel was dank and dim, I had not noticed it on the three occasions we had been to a service when the banns were read for our marriage. The grey January day cast little light through the small slit windows, the candle on the bare altar fluttered in the draught from a broken window, throwing an eerie, puny light on my bridegroom and I as we stood before a rotund priest at our marriage ceremony.

'I pronounce you man and wife,' the priest said in a mundane voice. Clarissa clapped her hands together at the priest's words, bringing to a conclusion such a dreary marriage service. I glanced sideways at my tall handsome husband, his face expressionless, his fair hair curling on the collar of his black frock coat. He glanced down at me and smiled.

'You look beautiful,' he whispered, although I never considered myself as beautiful, although some said that my grey eyes fringed by long curling dark lashes would attract any man.

I had known Kieran for four months and suddenly realised I knew so little about this man I had just married, except that he was thirty years old and lived in Wales where we were to travel this very day; and that was when the first rumblings of doubt came into my mind.

'Take my arm, Madam.' As he spoke in his deep measured voice, Kieran offered me the crook of his arm, I did as I was bid and we proceeded to walk down the aisle. As we stepped out of the chapel door into the yellow daylight large flakes of snow fell like pieces of white lace, adorning my beige-coloured cape which I pulled about my person, for I was cold from head to foot, my nose threatening to drip on to my cape.

As I watched the snow swirling down ever faster I recalled how I had dreamt of marrying a man I loved wearing white lace, so unlike the gown I wore today was my thought as I looked down at my beige-coloured poplin skirts which were already beginning to get wet on the hem, the snowflakes now settling on my black boots causing me to shiver.

'You are cold, Madam,' observed my husband solicitously. 'Let us get you into the carriage.' Before Kieran helped me into the carriage, Clarissa and I put our arms around each other as she kissed me on the cheek, and Kieran thanked Mrs Malvers. As I was helped up the steps of the carriage I suddenly felt sad and knew I was stepping into the unknown.

I made myself comfortable on the plush red velvet seats as Kieran wrapped a burgundy-coloured blanket around my legs. On looking around the carriage I could see my brown port-manteau containing all my worldly possessions had been placed on the corner of the seat.

Through the window I could see Clarissa waving at me. A tear slipped from my eye and trickled slowly down my cheek lingering on my mouth, a mouth my husband had never ventured to kiss, but he is after all, a gentleman. I chided myself as the carriage moved off.

My friend shouted, 'Good luck!' And I watched her and the chapel fade away in the distance until I could no longer see either my friend or the place Kieran and I had become husband and wife. Kieran leant across and took both of my hands in his.

'No regrets I hope, Mrs Alexander?' he said quietly.

'None.' I assured him, for it wasn't regrets that I had, but a niggling doubt at the back of my mind, and wondered with some misgivings where he was taking me to spend our first night together as man and wife.

The snow persisted during our journey, driving against the carriage, so much so that we could scarcely see out of the window. We stopped at a hostelry for some refreshment and when we stepped back into the carriage I could see the snow was banking up on each side of the track, and I set to wonder if we would safely reach our destination, but our cheery conversation lightened the journey.

'We are nearly there, wife,' Kieran's voice startled me as he had hardly spoken for the last half-hour. 'We will be at Rowan Castle in about ten minutes and not before time, I'm thinking. I've sent word ahead so we are expected, all will be waiting to meet my bride.'

'I am looking forward to seeing your home and meeting your family, I pray your castle isn't too grand for I am just a simple young woman,' I said pleasantly.

'You can see for yourself, Barbara.' As my husband spoke I could see through the driving snow that we had left the mountains behind and turning through some gates travelled up a long driveway flanked by trees, the bare branches of which were heavy with snow. In the distance I could make out a huge building with crenulated towers, the light from the candles already twinkling in many of the windows and smoke spiralling from the chimneys.

As we drew up to the main entrance I gave a gasp of surprise, it was very grand, but in this weather I could barely make anything out except to see that the walls were a sandy red and the vast expanse of the building boasted large mullioned windows.

'You are impressed, Mrs Alexander?' Kieran asked of me a smile on his lips.

'I am overawed, I had not expected . . .' I began and could say no more so overwhelmed was I by the immense size of my new home. As I looked one half of the main double doors opened and a woman with a lantern held high called out to us.

'Welcome home, brother, please hurry, I am anxious to greet your wife.'

As Kieran helped me from the carriage the woman stood at the top of the steps watching our progress towards her. I shielded my face with my hand against the biting snow, how I wished I didn't feel so weary, all I wanted to do was climb into a soft bed and lie between crisp white sheets, and then the thought came to me that this night I would not lie alone. Reaching the top of the steps I could see the woman with the lantern was as young as I, her fair curls were partly covered by a pale blue lace mantilla which matched the full skirts of her blue merino dress.

'Come,' she said taking my arm and drawing me through the main door into the vast hallway where I could see a fire burned cheerily in the huge stone fireplace with a pile of logs stacked against the wall. 'I am Justine,' the young woman continued, 'Kieran's only sister, welcome to Rowan and to the family. I shall be more than pleased to have your company.' As she spoke Justine placed the lantern on a chair and then proceed to untie the ribbons of my bonnet which she then removed to reveal my golden brown hair, passing the bonnet to a maid in a black dress with a white frilly apron covering it.

It was then that I saw the row of people waiting to greet me. My cheeks grew hot and all I wished for was to escape, having been so used to spending hours alone I found all these people quite intimidating.

'This,' said my sister-in-law stopping by a short buxom woman dressed in a grey serge dress with a white frilly cap covering her dark greying hair, 'is Mrs Burnet, our housekeeper.'

'It's lovely to meet you, mistress,' said Mrs Burnet taking one of my hands in both of hers and squeezing it gently, she smiled and her eyes twinkled and I knew that the housekeeper and I would get on well.

'I'm pleased to meet you,' I said quietly, still overawed by my surroundings. I felt I was in a dream and at any moment would awaken to find myself in the dingy room I had occupied in my lodgings near Shrewsbury Castle.

'Mrs Burnet will introduce you to the staff,' said Justine going back to my husband who stood watching me in silence and I set to wondering what he was thinking. Did he regret marrying me? His expression was unfathomable. While I had been in deep thought, Mrs Burnet and I had moved along the row of head maids and kitchen maids, six in all and then we reached the young woman at the end of the line who was dressed in black like the others with a white apron and a mob cap perched on her black curly hair.

'And this is Megan, Mrs Alexander,' said the housekeeper. I could sense she was fond of the girl who was about twenty.

'I'm pleased to meet you, mistress,' Megan said in a sweet Welsh accent, dropping me a curtsey at the same time.

'Megan is to be your personal maid mistress, she has many skills and is a friendly soul if this suits you,' enquired the housekeeper.

'I would be delighted, Megan,' I agreed, not wishing anyone to know I had not had a maid before.

'And I am Derrick Alexander.' A masculine voice from behind me startled me and I turned to see a tall man similar in stature to my husband Kieran and I guessed this to be the brother he had talked of. While Kieran was quiet his brother exuded friendliness his blue eyes dancing with merriment.

'I've heard a lot about you,' I said foolishly for I had no idea of what to say to anyone, I felt I had been thrown into a den of lions although the welcome I had been given was friendly enough.

'All good I hope,' said Derrick taking hold of my gloved hand and kissing the back of it and I thought once more that my bridegroom had not yet kissed me not even on this, our wedding day.

'And I am Kerensa Templeton.' Looking over Derrick's shoulder I could see the beautiful young woman who had spoken. She had not been in the hall when we arrived for I would not have missed her, her flaming red hair cascaded down the back of her emerald green silk cloak, underneath which she wore a matching dress, the bodice so tight at the waist it accentuated her perfect figure. I suddenly felt inadequate and hated this woman on sight as she looked me up and down, her green eyes flashing. Without a second glance in my direction she swept past me and headed for my husband whose face held a wary expression, but nonetheless his eyes lit up with pleasure at the sight of her.

'Kieran, darling!' enthused Kerensa, taking both my husband's hands in hers and kissing him on both cheeks. 'It is so good to have you back, Derrick has been a complete bore and won't go riding with me along the beach,' she complained beautifully.

'I don't think any of us will be riding for a while,' Derrick said, annoyance in his voice. 'There is a blizzard raging outside which could last for days.'

'How convenient,' Kerensa expressed her displeasure and slipped her arm through that of my husband. 'At least you are back, dear Kieran, that's all that matters to me.' She tossed her head, her hair rippling luxuriantly down her back, it was as if I wasn't there. I felt the tears well up in my eyes.

'You will join us for dinner?' asked Derrick.

'I think not,' I replied as I glanced at the beautiful but arrogant Kerensa Templeton. 'What I need is an early night.'

'Let me take you to your room,' interrupted the kindly housekeeper, 'for I can see it is rest you need, and we will have some refreshment sent up to you. Come now.'

I had not expected Kieran to be so indifferent to the fact that I had just become his wife, and I certainly hadn't expected him to be so attentive to the most lovely woman I had ever set eyes on. Even Justine had disappeared and I set to wondering if she had been disappointed by her brother's bride.

By the time we had walked along the wide corridor my whole body shivered with the cold and as Mrs Burnet ushered me into my room, tears were streaming down my face; unwilling tears for I had not wished to cry in front of anyone.

'There child,' the housekeeper soothed placing her arm around me and drawing me towards her ample bosom, 'you cry, let it out.' And I did, tears of pity for myself and the situation I had placed myself in. I had married without any mention of love and Clarissa's words came back to me, 'But you hardly know him, Barbara.' Suddenly I pushed myself away from Mrs Burnet's warm embrace, catching my hand on the keys at her waist causing them to jangle. I laughed and sobbed at the same time.

'I must make the most of this,' I said to Mrs Burnet, my tears subsided and I pulled myself up straight with determination, looking around at my surroundings. 'What a beautiful room.' I gasped, my tears forgotten as I looked around me. The drapes at the windows and around the huge four-poster bed which dominated the room were of red-coloured velvet, and crisp white sheets peeped over the red counterpane on the bed which looked inviting to one as weary as I.

'I'm so pleased, mistress, 'tis the master bedroom, where all the Alexander heirs have slept,' she informed me bustling over to a beige curtain in one corner of the room and as she drew it back I could see it had concealed a hip bath. 'Now I'll get some water sent up and we'll get you into a nice warm bath.'

As soon as she spoke Mrs Burnet removed my cape, draping it over a small chair which stood by the window and then she bade me to sit on a comfortable beige-coloured armchair which was drawn up to the fire. Sitting down I put my feet on the fender and bent to remove my boots while the housekeeper went off on her mission for water. I was warming my hands by the fire and feeling more relaxed than I had all day when there was a knock on my door. My heart thudded thinking it was my husband, but surely he wouldn't knock.

'Come in.' I called in as strong a

voice as I could muster. The door opened to reveal a pleasant-looking middle-aged man who had brought up my portmanteau.

'Where would you like it, mistress?' he asked in a kindly Welsh brogue.

'Somewhere by the wardrobe, please,' I answered, pointing to the large mahogany wardrobe which stood against a wall by the window.

'There you are,' he said as he placed my possessions where I had indicated. 'I'm David, the housekeeper's husband, if there's anything I can do for you, you have only to ask.'

'Thank you, David, that's very kind of you, I'll remember it,' I assured him.

The water for my bath was brought up and I sank thankfully into the warmth of it. Megan helped me out, wrapping me in a fluffy white towel, luxuries I had never been used to and I recalled the cracked jug and bowl I had washed in at my lodgings, quite often with cold water.

'Are you to dress in your nightgown,

mistress?' asked Megan as I dried myself.

'Yes, I think that is the best course to take.' I agreed, although I did now feel more alert.

'Is it all right for me to unpack your luggage?' my maid asked.

'Why yes, but I've not much to unpack as you will see,' I replied somewhat ruefully.

'The master's first wife had little when she first arrived, but if she's anything to go by you'll have a wardrobe full of pretty things before too long.'

Megan's words drifted across to me and stopped me in my tracks.

'The master's first wife?' I said with some astonishment, reiterating my maids words. 'So my husband has been wed before?' I asked with great interest.

'Yes indeed. I'm sorry mistress, I thought you knew.' Megan apologised, an anguished look on her face.

'No matter,' I soothed for I could see the girl was quite distraught. 'I'm glad you told me for I would have learned of it soon enough.'

Megan had taken my best white lawn nightdress out of my bag, I had pressed it only this morning when I had high hopes of a happy wedding day. But since our arrival at Rowan Castle the day had not gone well, indeed not, and as Megan slipped the nightgown over my head and fastened the pearl buttons I tried not to anticipate how my wedding night would fair.

Sitting at the dressing table, Megan brushed my long straight golden brown hair until it shone. The reflection which looked back at me was pleasant enough, but I had not one ounce of the beauty Kerensa Templeton possessed. At the thought of her I felt angry at the way both she and my husband had acted as if I weren't there, as if I hadn't this very day married the master of Rowan Castle.

'What was the master's first wife called?' I asked Megan, startling the girl as the only sound in the room for some time had been the logs crackling on the fire.

'Annabel,' was Megan's short answer.

'And what happened to the first Mrs Alexander?' I asked quietly, needing to know more about my predecessor.

'It's not for me to say, mistress,' the girl answered quietly, the hairbrush still in her hand. 'The housekeeper would be the one to ask.'

'Very well, Megan, but you can see I have a right to know,' I said, meeting her eyes in the mirror.

'Oh yes, you certainly have and I hope you find out soon,' she said, as a look of sympathy mirrored in her lovely brown eyes. 'I'll unpack the rest of your things now if that's all right with you?' she asked of me.

'Thank you, Megan.'

I was very interested in my husband's first wife and I set to wondering if the reason he had been so aloof to me since we had arrived at Rowan Castle was because he felt a traitor to her memory. But my instinct was that he was head over heels in love with the beautiful Kerensa. Whatever the situation my intention was to find out exactly where she fitted into the scheme of things at Rowan Castle. I chided myself, I must be tired to even think these things about my beloved Kieran.

After my maid had left I crossed over to the window and pulled back one of the heavy curtains. Snow had started to bank up on the window pane, but over it I could see the blizzard still driving down and the white landscape looked like a huge cake topped with icing sugar. Swiftly I drew the curtain back in place, the whole scene causing me to feel cold once more.

For a little while I sat by the fire thinking of the day's events, it all still felt like a dream, our wedding, the castle, its inhabitants and the heavy snowfall all seemed unreal and for an instant Derrick's smiling face appeared in my mind.

I glanced at the clock on the mantle which showed the time to be nearly midnight. Would my bridegroom come to me or was he with the lovely Miss Templeton? I blew out the candle on the table by my chair and climbed between the crisp white sheets, my honey brown hair spread on the snow white pillow. By the candle light I looked around the room lying expectantly waiting for some time, but as I suspected Kieran did not appear. I couldn't honestly say if I was relieved or disappointed, but whatever I felt it would appear for tonight at least I was to sleep in the marriage bed alone.

2

I awoke refreshed the next morning after a surprisingly good night's sleep in the comfortable four-poster bed. Megan was already in the room, she had lit the fire and drawn back the heavy curtains to reveal a watery sunlight casting its ray across the carpeted floor. I got out of bed with a resolution to be strong today and face my husband with a clear and firm determination. Little did I know this was to be easier said than done.

As I slipped out of bed I noticed things I had not seen the previous evening. To one side of the bed I observed a doorway draped with a red curtain which hung from a brass pole.

'Good morning, mistress,' Megan distracted me, 'It's a better morning, at least the snow has stopped falling,' she said in a cheery voice, at her words I stepped over to the window. The snowfall had indeed ceased, the whole countryside was covered in a blanket of white as were the mountains beyond. I walked back to the fire warming my hands in front of the blazing coals.

'I need to look my best today, Megan,' I said, turning to her as she poured water from a jug into the china bowl.

'We'll make you fit for a king,' replied Megan, throwing me a beautiful smile and I set to thinking she must know I slept alone, but I felt I couldn't breach the delicate subject with her, to me it was embarrassing and I needed to know the young woman better before I could confide in her.

Megan had just finished twisting my hair into a knot and securing it with pins when Justine walked in.

'I've come to take you down to breakfast, Barbara,' she said. All the while glancing around the room, her eyes resting on the marital bed. It was plain for her to see that only one side had been slept in. 'Run along Megan please, I wish to talk to your mistress.'

Megan did as she was bid and Justine waited until the door had closed behind her before she spoke again. 'All is not well is it, Barbara?' As she spoke Justine looked at me expectantly, waiting for an answer.

'No, it is not,' I said calmly moving away from the dressing table.

'What is amiss? For Kieran has been in the library since six o'clock this morning.' As she spoke she glanced again at the four-poster and then back to me.

'In truth, Justine, I don't know what is amiss,' I answered her, looking out over the landscape.

'I will not interfere, for now at least,' Justine began, 'we shall go down to breakfast and then I will show you around your new home. We are to hope that things will improve and . . . ' Here she looked me up and down. 'You look charming, but as soon as the snow disappears we will take a trip to

Llanberis to see Mrs Harding the local dressmaker.'

So, I thought, it was very probably Justine who had arranged the first Mrs Alexander's wardrobe, did this mean that Annabel had little in the way of possessions also? This to me was a very intriguing question. As I walked with Justine along the corridor and down the staircase with the wide curving polished banister I mulled this over in my mind.

On reaching the hall I glanced around, so tired had I been the night before I had taken no heed of my surroundings on entering the castle.

'The building is fourteenth century,' Justine told me as I looked at the large tapestries depicting hunting scenes which hung on the whitewashed stone walls. The floorboards beneath my feet were of dark wood and highly polished, candle sconces were dotted around the walls with the odd reindeer head here and there, the antlers curling majestically.

'The hall has a lot of character,' I

observed as I followed Justine to a corridor which led off the hallway. The door of the room we entered was open and as I stepped inside the first thing I saw was the huge table of light polished wood which could seat at least sixteen people. My heart sank as I saw Kerensa Templeton seated at the head of the table eating her breakfast.

She turned around giving me a cursory glance before returning her attention back to her plate. Thankfully Derrick was there also, he stood up and pushed back his chair when he saw me, quite the gentleman was my thought. I was somewhat relieved to see that Kieran was not there, and then I chided myself that it was how I felt.

At Justine's direction I lifted each silver lid on the dishes laid out on the huge sideboard, helping myself to breakfast. I sat down opposite Derrick who gave me an encouraging smile whilst Justine poured me coffee.

'Where is Keiran?' said Kerensa in a sweet voice to no-one in particular.

'Where indeed,' the words escaped my lips unwittingly.

'She has a voice!' Kerensa said in a cutting tone.

'Don't be rude,' Justine admonished her. 'Barbara is the mistress now, so you'd do well to curb your tongue, young woman.'

'So you've lost him have you?' Kerensa said to me, ignoring Justine's advice completely. 'Or maybe you never really found him.' And she laughed, a light laugh, but it was meant to accompany her unkind words.

'You are wrong there, Miss Templeton,' I retorted, my knife and fork poised in my hands, 'for I can assure you Kieran and I married only yesterday.'

'Married!' Kerensa shrieked. 'It's just a word, for it will never last.'

'It might be better for all, Kerensa, if you kept your misjudged opinions to yourself for once,' cut in Derrick, who had been watching the two of us waiting for the right moment to interrupt. Kerensa's answer was to push back her chair and flounce out of the room, the skirts of her exquisite pale-blue gown swishing on the patterned carpet, but before leaving she turned back in the doorway and said, 'You'll see, I'm right,' and left us with the sound of her laughter ringing in our ears.

'Don't fret about her,' soothed Derrick, laying a hand across mine on the table as though it were the most natural thing to do, 'she has always been the same since we were children.'

'So she lives here and always has?' I asked.

'Kerensa is our late father's ward,' explained Justine, 'she is the daughter of a good friend who died when Kerensa was a small child. She is twenty-two now and free to leave having been left a vast inheritance, but she chooses not to go . . . '

'Because of Kieran,' I finished the sentence for her and neither Derrick nor Justine contradicted me.

After breakfast Justine told me to wait in the hall while she instructed Ginny, the head maid, to clear the dining table. I was looking closely at a particularly attractive tapestry when Kieran's voice startled me.

'Good morning, Barbara, I trust you slept well,' he said as if nothing was wrong and he hadn't totally ignored me since our arrival. I walked across to him.

'Why did you not join me in our room last night?' I asked quietly for I failed to understand it.

'Believe me when I say I have good reason,' Kieran replied gently, a smile curving his perfect mouth.

'What has happened to you since we arrived here?' I asked. 'You suddenly seem cold and distant, where as in Shrewsbury you were charming and attentive. Do you not find me attractive anymore?' The thought had suddenly occurred to me.

'Have no fear, Barbara, I find you endearing. But I cannot share a room with you for the time being at least. And when I do I shall arrive through the adjoining door.' At his words I recalled seeing the doorway alongside my bed.

'Then I shall lock it,' I said with triumph, at the same time loathing the words I spoke for I yearned for Kieran to need me as a wife.

'You do as you will, Barbara, but I ask that you have patience with me.' As he spoke he touched my cheek gently and then walked off in the directions of the dining-room.

It wasn't usual for me to stamp my foot with frustration, but I did only to be caught out by Mrs Burnet as she walked across the hallway closely followed by Justine.

'Is it the master?' they both said in unison.

'It most certainly is,' was my emphatic reply to the question. 'Mrs Burnet, I wish the door between my bedroom and my husband's to be locked forthwith.'

'Surely not,' said Justine, aghast to think that I should be barring her brother from my room.

'I don't wish to speak of it,' I said with a strength I didn't feel. 'Now please show me my new home as you promised.'

Justine took me to see the morning-room first which was a pleasant room, quite small compared with the dining-room and decorated in pale green, with green brocade curtains at the windows beyond which I could see the snow, the watery sun not having any effect on the white scene. There was a charming writing desk standing beneath the window.

'You can write your letters here,' said Justine with some enthusiasm and I could tell that she liked this room.

'I only have one person to write to,' I admitted honestly, 'For I am an orphan and only recently left my position as teacher where I worked my fingers to the bone in the kitchens also. I had very little time for social pursuits.'

'That's strange . . . ' commended Justine.

'What is?' I asked looking at her for she had a thoughtful expression on her face.

'Nothing really, I suppose,' my sister-in-law began, 'it's just that Annabel was an orphan also with no-one, but it's nothing. Come now, I want to show you the ballroom.'

'You mean Kieran's first wife, don't you?' I said quietly.

'Yes, but come now, that's all in the past.'

Although it was in the past, the fact that my husband had been wed before and not had the decency to tell me very much affected the present, along with the lovely Kerensa. Kieran had all the cards stacked against him as far as I was concerned. But I said no more and followed Kieran's sister along the corridor until we reached an archway with no door.

We entered the largest room I had ever seen, not even the assembly room at the academy had been so vast. I looked around me, the bottom half of the walls were panelled in a rich coloured wood giving the room a feeling of warmth even though no fire burned in the large stone fireplace, which was set in the wall opposite the four windows, at which hung red curtains with gold braided tassels looping them back from the glass.

The floor was of polished wood and completely clear of furniture, except for beautiful red and gold brocade chairs which stood side by side against the panelling. Large portraits covered the walls above and over the fireplace I caught sight of a painting which drew me to it.

So out of place was it amongst the faces of the Alexander ancestors, I went to stand before it in the centre of the room so as to get the full effect of the beauty of it. The subject matter was a waterfall which flowed down between craggy rocks, falling on the boulders beneath, it was so real I almost believed

I stood in front of it in reality.

'It is rather beautiful, isn't it,' observed Justine as she came over to stand beside me. 'It is a picture of Rowan Falls, from where I believe the castle got its name being only a small way from here. Kieran has been fascinated by the falls ever since he was a child. I've no doubt he will take you to see them when the weather improves.'

I couldn't have known it then, but Rowan Falls would play a great part in my life and in some ways shape my future.

'It is beautiful as you say,' I agreed, 'and I'm sure the reality surpasses the beauty of the painting.' As I spoke I found it difficult to draw my eyes away but Justine had more pressing things on her mind.

'This is where we shall hold a ball to celebrate your marriage to my brother,' she enthused. 'All the gentry from hereabouts will be invited and we will dance until dawn in your honour.'

'There is really nothing to celebrate, for now at least,' I said, dampening my sister-in-law's spirits.

'Give it time, Barbara,' she said placing her arm around my shoulder. 'I would wager that by the time the snow has disappeared all will be well.'

Sometime later back in my room, darkness was falling and I thought of her words. I knew in my heart that things would one day be well between Kieran and I. Going across to the doorway by my bed, I drew back the curtain and tried the handle of the door.

Thankfully it was shut firmly against my husband.

Mrs Burnet had very obviously heeded my instructions. The only light in the room was from the flames of the fire which leapt up the chimney. I couldn't locate the tapers to light the candles and while I waited for Megan I walked across to the window, the view outside was akin to a haunted land-scape with a silver moon casting its light on the snow.

Everything was still and quiet, how eerie it looked, I mused and shuddered once more at the sight of it. Megan did not appear so I headed back down the stairs to see Justine crossing the hall.

'Justine,' I called to her, she looked up a startled smile on her face.

'Can I help?' she asked.

'Have you a work basket with needle and threads please, as I have a sampler to complete, but nothing to work with,' I told her.

'Why yes, there is one in the morning room which belonged to my mother,' she offered. 'Can you find your own way for I am about to speak to the cook about the menu for dinner tomorrow. I know it should be your job but best you settle in first.'

'I shall find my way,' I assured her and as she started to walk on I interrupted her progress. 'By the by Justine, I wish to see the dressmaker at the earliest opportunity if that can be arranged.'

'But of course, dear,' Justine agreed. 'We shall go as soon as the tracks are clear.'

Making my way to the morning room I was quite proud of myself, for once in my life I felt as if I was in control of the situation. I acknowledged that I needed finer clothes, in some small way to enhance my appearance. I suddenly had a spring in my step and entered the morning room with renewed determination.

I located the workbox which stood on the floor by the writing desk, it was a wooden box, quite small in size with a handle. On lifting the lid I could see an array of coloured threads, red, green, blue and yellow to name but a few, with needles and pin cushions plus a delightful silver thimble. Placing it on my finger I was delighted to see it fitted perfectly.

About to close the lid of the workbox I stopped for I could see a name inscribed in the wood, looking closer I could see the name, Annabel. My heart sank. So Justine had lied to me and if this was the case, what else had she lied about if anything?

Nevertheless, I closed the lid and catching hold of the handle proceeded back to the hallway. As I reached the doorway I stopped in my tracks as I could hear voices, one of them was certainly Kerensa, standing to the side of the doorway I carefully peered into the candlelit hall. It was Kieran she was with and their voices drifted across to me.

'But why did you marry her, darling when you could have married me?' said Kerensa's pleading voice.

'Because Kerensa, I have told you so many times I cannot marry you,' said my husband in a gentle voice.

At these words Kerensa entwined her arms around his neck and he bent his head as if to kiss her lips. My heart thudded for I felt like an intruder, but to my astonishment he gently pushed her away from him, as they drew apart the lovely Miss Templeton said softly, so softly I could only just hear her words, 'But darling, she is a mouse.'

'Don't be unkind, Kerensa,' were my husband's words.

I fled back to the morning room, my heart racing. I would show my husband and Miss Kerensa Templeton that I could indeed be anything but a mouse.

3

Sunday morning arrived and so did Justine just as Megan was arranging my hair. I knew we were to attend chapel today in the grounds of the castle, for Justine had told me only yesterday.

'Good morning, Barbara,' my sister-in-law said cheerily as she looked at Megan.

'It's all right, Miss,' said Megan to Justine, 'I'll just finish securing this pin and I'll be gone.' My maid obviously sensed that Justine wished to speak with me alone.

'How are you today?' Justine asked of me. 'And is there an improvement in your relationship with my brother?'

'Sadly no,' I answered, 'if it weren't for Kerensa I feel there may be a chance.'

'Why do you say that?' asked Kieran's sister.

'Because Justine, I saw them together in the hall last evening,' I told her honestly, recalling last night's incident.

What I failed to comprehend were Kieran's words, 'Because I cannot marry you.' it was a very strange thing to say; little did I know that in the weeks ahead I would come to understand it.

'No matter now,' said Justine dismissing the problem, 'I've come to ask you if you would like to choose one of my gowns to wear to chapel today?' she asked looking at my dull brown dress.

'I couldn't,' I uttered, the proud part of me coming to the surface.

'I understand how you feel, but whatever you choose you are welcome to keep. I have gowns aplenty and it would tide you over until we are able to visit Mrs Harding, the dressmaker,' Justine said kindly.

'Very well,' I agreed, for I knew that to go to the chapel in my present gown meant I would feel akin to one of the servants, who I knew from Megan would attend the morning service.

'Splendid, come along to my room where we can assess the situation.' Doing as I was bid I followed Justine further along the corridor and around a corner where we entered a smaller bedroom than mine, which was in truth a very feminine one, everything was pink, the heavy damask curtains, the bed hangings, the carpet and wallpaper boasting large pink roses, and the figurines dotted here and there on the mantel and small table were pink also.

The only thing not pink was the white marble fireplace from which a fire burned lazily in the hearth. I stepped over to where Justine was opening her large wardrobe door, I gasped at the sight of its contents. Gowns of all hues and colours and various materials hung closely together.

'This side of the wardrobe is where my winter gowns are hung,' Justine told me, and I could see some were darker in colour. My eyes rested on a wine-coloured velvet gown with a white sable collar. 'You have chosen I can tell,' said my sister-in-law. 'Now tell me which one your eyes have alighted on for at last I can see a sparkle in their depths.'

I laughed as I lifted out the gown, it was sumptuous and heavy and would no doubt keep me warm. The skirts were full and the back of the jacket fell over the skirts to a point, the buttoned bodice nipping in at the waist and the white sable sitting snugly at the neckline.

'Can I really have this one?' I asked.

'Yes indeed, you have good taste, Barbara. Now let us get you into it,' ordered my sister-in-law, already helping me out of my brown merino day dress. As I slipped into the velvet jacket, the material of the sleeves felt luxurious on my bare skin, the white sable at the wrists feeling soft and warm. Justine walked me over to a full-length mirror set in the wardrobe door.'

'It's beautiful!' I enthused, 'And the colours so rich and warm looking.

Thank you,' I said and gave Justine a well deserved hug. Never had I been dressed in something so sumptuous and expensive, indeed gazing at the reflection of myself in the mirror, the image looking back at me didn't seem like me at all.

'Here,' said Justine as she passed me a white beaded reticule, 'this will finish the whole thing off admirably.'

'As indeed it does,' I agreed, looking briefly once more at my reflection.

'It is 10.45,' said Justine with some alarm, 'we must assemble in the hall, but not before I give you this,' she said reaching in a hatbox and then coming across to me. I looked with some delight at the beautiful bonnet which she then placed on my head. The wine velvet matched my gown, the wide brim edged with white sable looked perfection as Justine tied the white ribbons around my neck.

As we walked back along the corridor my sister-in-law in a rose-pink gown and cloak with a matching bonnet on her fair curls, I felt like a queen. As we stepped down the staircase into the hall I felt a different person from the plain, simple, uneasy young woman who had arrived at Rowan Castle only three days ago.

The other three members of the household were already waiting in the hall, my husband looking as handsome and immaculate as ever in a black frock coat, as was his brother Derrick, who as I watched them talking I could see was a little taller than Kieran. Kerensa was dressed like a bride I thought, in a cream-coloured gown and cloak of shimmering satin, her glorious red wavy hair tied back with a matching ribbon, she looked a picture of perfection I realised, and knew that no matter what I dressed in I could never match her beauty.

Her green eyes flashed with a look of surprise as she saw me, just at the moment Kieran took notice I was there and a spark of the man I had married showed in his blue eyes, but was as quickly gone to be replaced by a look of indifference towards me.

'Take my arm, wife,' he said unexpectedly, and I did as I was bid without any conscious thought, and glancing at Kerensa I could see the scowl of her face which for an instant marred her beauty, and I felt pleased with myself, pleased that I was Kieran's wife and that it was I who held his arm.

The small building where we were to worship was built of the same large sandy red stone as the castle, set back at the side of it. When we stepped into the interior I had a sudden intake of breath for the chapel wasn't as austere as I had expected it to be. It was charming in its simplicity, carved wood panelling covered the bottom half of the whitewashed walls, ahead of us over the altar was an exquisite stained-glass window, which held my attention as Kieran and I took our places in the front pew.

The congregation complete, which included Megan, the housekeeper and her husband, David, the service commenced. Kerensa who sat on a pew on the other side of the aisle kept glancing across to look at Kieran with a distracted expression on her lovely face.

I felt elated that I was with my husband as we stepped out into the fresh air once Kieran took my arm, and I could see that the lovely Miss Templeton was irate at this. We left her standing there like an abandoned child.

'Walk with me,' came Derrick's voice as he took Kerensa's arm. And as I turned back to look, I could see an unattractive scowl on the young woman's face; whereas my heart was singing and as I clasped my husband's arm tighter he looked down at me and smiled.

Later on in my room, removing the exquisite bonnet and placing it on the bed, something caused me to go over and try the connecting door, some instinct made me do it and as I tried the handle the door flew open to reveal Kieran's very masculine bedroom, which was decorated in colours of brown and beige.

Swiftly I closed the door, I was incensed and set off along the corridor and down the staircase in search of Mrs Burnet. I was directed to the house-keeper's quarters by Ginny, who looked somewhat startled at my sudden over-bearing manner, but I gave little thought to this as I walked down a clean but shabby narrow corridor to the room the head maid had directed me to.

I knocked on the door and David's voice called for me to enter, both he and his wife seemed startled to see me.

'Why mistress!' said Mrs Burnet in a shocked manner, 'Whatever ails you? Do come and sit down, you look as white as a sheet,' she said, urging me to sit on a small red chair.

'I'm sorry to intrude, Mrs Burnet,' I apologised, watching David as he sat on a chair by the small dining table lighting his pipe, this fascinated me and I must have watched him too intently for the housekeeper walked over to him and took the pipe from his mouth saying, 'Don't smoke in front of the young mistress, David. Now go and make her a nice cup of tea,' she instructed her husband. David left the room through a doorway into what must have led to a scullery for I could hear the kettle being filled with water.

'Now while my David is gone, you tell me what's amiss,' she said sitting opposite me and taking one of my hands in hers.

'The door in my room,' I began, 'it's unlocked once more.' At my words, Mrs Burnet looked at me with sympathy in her eyes.

'I'm sorry, mistress Barbara, truly I am,' she said squeezing my hand, 'but the master ordered me to unlock it.'

'Well, I'm asking you now to lock it again,' I instructed her. 'Please lock it and give me the key, that's the best idea,' I said suddenly feeling much better at this wonderful notion of mine, for if I had the key no-one could unlock it again.

'Well, you're the mistress without a doubt,' agreed Mrs Burnet releasing my hand and going over to her bunch of keys which I could see hung on a large hook by the fireplace. She brought them over to me and after a struggle released the said key and handed it to me just as David brought in a tray of tea and biscuits which he deposited on a small table by his wife's chair.

'There you are, Pegs,' he said, 'while you're taking tea with the mistress, I'll go and clear some snow before darkness falls.'

Left on our own, Mrs Burnet poured some tea.

'It's not really my place to say, mistress, but I can see you're unhappy about something, and that grieves me to see that you are in this large castle with hardly a friend to your name,' she said kindly.

'I'm used to being alone, for hours at a time on occasions, Mrs Burnet,' I told her.

'I know it's not the done thing, but

when we are on our own I'd be so pleased if you'd call me Peggy, the last mistress did.' Here she stopped and I interrupted her train of thought.

'What exactly happened to Annabel?' I asked her, snatching the chance. 'Megan said you'd tell me.'

'It was a rare accident that befell the master's first wife,' began Peggy Burnet. I smiled at her encouragingly as she continued, 'The poor girl slipped and fell at the waterfall into the water below, her body has never been found.'

'So how do you know what happened?' I queried.

'Because the master was there. He did all he could to save her by all accounts, but it was in vain. Right sorry I was as she was a lovely young woman, a bit like you, she even looked like you in some ways, but now she's gone.' And the housekeeper looked ahead of her with her own private thoughts.

'And was she happy? Annabel I mean.' For I needed to know the answer to this important question.

'She was very happy, lit up the whole place with her smile, and yet there was something not quite right, now and then she would have a faraway look on her face.'

'And did they marry here at the castle?' Was my next question.

'Bless me no, mistress. The master brought her back one day, just like he did you, but with a couple of hours warning.' Here she stopped and I wondered if I could press her farther.

'And how long were they together before this unfortunate accident?' I asked.

'About two months would be my reckoning,' Mrs Burnet told me. 'But don't you go dwelling on all that I've told you, mistress. I just want you to be happy, a young woman like you deserves some joy in life. Look at me, I've been married to my David for nigh on thirty years.'

Walking back across the large hallway I encountered Derrick. 'Barbara, we have been looking for you, everyone is waiting for you to join us in the drawing-room for our weekly evening of music,' he told me.

'I would prefer to go to my room,' I said, the key to the communicating door burning in the pocket of my velvet skirt. I desperately wished to lock the door before Kieran went to his room for the night.

'Please join us, Barbara, it would please me to have my beautiful young sister-in-law for company,' Derrick cajoled me.

'As you asked so sweetly I will join you for a short while,' I agreed as Derrick put his hand beneath my elbow and steered me towards the drawing-room, somewhere I'd not been before.

On entering the room, the first person I saw was Kerensa sitting on a stool by an upright piano which was beautifully made of walnut.

My thoughts drifted back to Kerensa, she had removed her cloak, the creamy white of her skin almost matched her gown and her hair now flowed freely once more down her back. It was an uncharitable thought, but I knew that if Miss Templeton could play the piano, I could play it as well as her, since I was a young child I had played and I loved music.

'Barbara!' exclaimed Justine, who sat on a cream settle by the magnificent onyx fireplace. The whole of the large room was impressive, most of the room was in cream, including the curtains which gave a light airy feel to the room, the tables and sideboards were in contrast of dark wood which the cream colour complimented perfectly. 'Where have you been?' Justine asked for the second time.

'I hope you don't mind, but I've been getting to know our housekeeper better,' I told her.

'What you do here is entirely of your own making, dear, as after all you are the mistress of Rowan Castle.' Did I detect some displeasure in Justine's voice I thought just as we were interrupted by Kerensa.

'Come and play for us, Barbara,' she

said, 'for I'm sure you can.' The young woman was being far too sweet, obviously hoping I could not play the piano.

'Very well,' I agreed walking over and asking Kerensa to vacate the stool, which she did with a swish of her skirts on the cream carpet beneath us. Kerensa walked over to Kieran purposefully, taking hold of his arm and kissing him on the cheek. I was anything but jealous, but for some reason the whole scene incensed me. Out of the corner of my eye I saw Derrick smile and wink at me with encouragement.

The beautiful music of Chopin filled the room and I felt vibrant and alive as I caressed the cream-coloured keys. I must have played for half-an-hour and could see that my husband, Derrick and Justine were enraptured by my performance, but Miss Templeton wore a scowl on her face once more as she tried to distract Kieran from my playing, but my husband would have none of it and stayed focused on me and my music the whole time, a look of pleasure on his handsome face.

I finished the piece with a flourish and bowed as they all clapped in unison, all except Kerensa who fidgeted and tried once more to hold Kieran's arm. I felt that this at last was my triumph over her and she was probably wishing she had not asked me to play, but my triumph was not to last.

Leaving the others in the drawing-room I went back to my room, noting how the candles cast a golden light along the corridor and looking out through one of the long arched windows I could see the scene outside was not so sparkling white even though the moon shone down on it.

Reaching my room and swiftly walking over to the connecting door, I locked it. I had a sudden hesitation for after the look on Kieran's face as I played Chopin I had a sudden indecision as to whether I really wanted to lock him out.

I was drifting off to sleep and wondering where Megan was when I heard footsteps in the hallway, they stopped and I heard a door quietly open. I felt sure it was Kieran and walked quietly to my door and out into the corridor along to my husband's room. As I reached it I could see the door was ajar and as I looked through the opening to my astonishment I could see Kerensa silhouetted in the moonlight.

As I watched, Kerensa sat on the bed and ran her hand lightly over the cover and pillows, as if in a caress. She then got up, walking gracefully over to the window and looking down on to the scene below, her lovely hair shining in the light from the moon. I wondered what her thoughts were as she stood there. Of unrequited love maybe, I mused.

As she went to turn back to the door I left as silently as I could and as I reached my room I heard the click of the door as Kerensa shut it.

As I lay in bed that night, a cloak of darkness surrounding me I mulled over the day's events. I heard the handle to the connecting door being turned in vain, but it did not bother me for both my doors were locked. Or did it bother me? No matter how cool Kieran had been with me since our arrival at the castle I was still desperately in love with him.

4

Three days passed and the snow disappeared, leaving behind an unfamiliar landscape. Sitting by the drawing room window stitching my sampler I could see two sweeping lawns, one each side of a narrow path led down to the surrounding wall of the castle.

Observing the mountains beyond, the peaks of which were still covered with snow, Justine's voice interrupted my thoughts, 'I thought I may find you here,' she said as she came across and looked down at my work. 'You've nearly completed it,' she said. I'd worked the sampler of linen with coloured silks for some time, the theme was the academy where I taught, surrounded by birds, trees and flowers.

A simple enough scene, so much so that a child of twelve could have done it, but embroidery was not one of my strong points. Justine had interrupted me as I stitched my name, Barbara Thorpe in red silk at the bottom, but of course my name was Alexander now I mused although I felt no different. 'You found the workbox,' observed Justine, indicating the wooden box on the floor at my feet.

'Yes, I found it, but it's not your mother's,' I told her.

'What makes you say that, Barbara?' Justine said, obviously quite taken aback by my words.

'Because Annabel's name is inside the lid,' I explained, lifting the workbox on to my lap and opening the lid for her to see.

'My mother's name was Annabel,' she told me in a voice which was barely a whisper. My heart thudded in my chest as I realised what an awful mistake I had made.

'I'm so sorry,' I said placing the workbox and my sampler on the chair as I went over to put an arm around Justine's shoulders for I could see she was upset. 'I understood Annabel to be Kieran's first wife.'

'She was, but it was also our mother's name,' she explained. 'That's why we thought it such a coincidence that Kieran should marry our mother's namesake.'

'I'm truly repentant, believe me,' I assured her.

'You weren't to know,' she told me gently, 'You've heard snippets of conversation from the servants no doubt and just haven't pieced it together very well.'

'No indeed I haven't,' I said sheepishly. 'I wouldn't normally make a judgment before holding the true facts in my hand. But Kieran has told me so little and in truth been so distant since we arrived here, I have pieced things together as you say and not made a very good task of it.'

'No matter,' said Justine in her normal voice, 'I've come to say that if you are agreeable we will visit Mrs Harding the dressmaker today.'

'That would be totally acceptable to me,' I agreed.

'Then shall we say ten o'clock? I will organise the carriage,' Justine told me as she walked to the drawing room door. Turning back her departing words were, 'Please give Kieran a chance for he has never got over the loss of his mother, nor his first wife.'

Justine left me wondering how the first Annabel departed this life and also my sister-in-law obviously had no notion of the liaison between her brother and his father's ward, and if she did she chose to ignore it. Or was I over-reacting?

Leaving my sampler and workbox on the chair, I made my way to my room to change into the wine-coloured velvet for my outing with Justine. As I reached the door of my husband's bedroom, he stepped into the corridor.

'Barbara,' he greeted me in an affable manner and, as I looked past him into his room beyond, I thought of the evening I had seen Kerensa silhouetted in the moonlight.

'Sir,' I returned in not so agreeable a manner.

'I wished to seek you out,' he continued, 'for I wish to show you Rowan Falls, a favourite beauty spot of mine. Do you ride?' he then asked and my heart somersaulted, here was another pursuit which Kerensa no doubt excelled in, and a pursuit that I had never had a chance to master.

'Sadly no,' I told him expecting a rebuffle. But his next words surprised me.

'Then I shall teach you, but in the meantime you will ride bareback behind me on my horse, Lancelot.' At his words I felt totally apprehensive.

'Very well.' And why I had agreed so amicably I couldn't honestly say, except to be with him alone again would bring joy to my heart.

'Tomorrow then, about 10.30,' Kieran suggested and as I watched his impressive figure striding down the corridor I could barely believe that this encounter had gone so well.

Duly attired with Megan's help, Justine and I set off to Llanberis in the carriage. Sitting once more on the plush red velvet seat of the carriage, Justine opposite me, dressed today in a cornflower blue outfit which suited her fair colouring admirably, I thought of my journey from Shrewsbury in the blizzard and the events that had happened in the short space of time I'd been at Rowan Castle.

We travelled through impressive mountainous countryside once more and Justine pointed out Mount Snowdon, the highest of mountains which I gazed at, in awe of the snow covered peak. As we climbed up through the pass I was exuberant at the changing scenery, from green grass to huge boulders of slate, which had at some time fallen to the ground beneath and lay in confusion at the feet of the mountains.

We left the mountains behind and travelled along a road lined with cottages opposite a pleasant lake and came to a halt outside a nicely cream painted double-fronted building with large windows either side of the dark blue front door. As Justine pulled the bell it was no time before the door opened to reveal Mrs Harding herself, a dour thin middle-aged woman who in view of the expensive gowns she made was dressed very plainly in brown which boasted a delightful cream lace collar.

'I'm pleased to meet you, Mrs Alexander,' the dressmaker said in a friendly manner as Justine introduced me. My sister-in-law and I looked through bales of beautifully-coloured material, from silks to velvet. I chose enough for four day dresses and four evening gowns in different shades from pale lemon to cornflower blue. I'd spotted a beautiful turquoise-coloured silk which I was drawn to.

'Your ballgown would be admirable in this,' Justine told me as Mrs Harding agreed.

'It is a glorious colour,' I said. 'Yes. If

you could please make a gown in the turquoise I'd be most pleased.'

As Justine and I travelled back to Rowan Castle through the mountains, I thought that to wear such a beautiful gown to the ball would compensate and more for the sad state of my marriage.

As we swept up the long drive I marvelled once more at the size of the sandy red castle which I was now mistress of.

'Is the whole of the castle in use?' I asked Justine.

'No, the wing on the left which is where our father and mother's quarters were is now uninhabited. In truth, my mother's room is as she left it,' she said wistfully. And as we came to a halt at the foot of the curving stone steps I wondered what Justine had meant when she spoke the words, 'As my mother left it.' I took it to mean her mother's passing from this world to the next and thought no more of it until some time later.

We could see another carriage pulled

in farther along the front of the castle, a plain black one, not half as magnificent as the one we had travelled in today. 'I wonder who that is,' Justine said, and as we entered the vast hallway, the fire burning in the grate, we were to find out when Mrs Burnet came running towards us.

'Mistress, Miss, thank the Lord you are home, the authorities are in the drawing room with the master,' she said breathlessly.

'And why is that?' said Justine, already removing her gloves and bonnet and patting her blonde curls into place.

'It would seem, Miss, they've found mistress Annabel,' Peggy Burnet informed us, reaching for the lace hanky in her pocket and dabbing her eyes with it.

'Thank you, Mrs Burnet, you may leave us. Quickly Barbara,' she said to me, 'remove your bonnet. You needn't come into the drawing room if you don't wish to,' she said as an after thought.

'No, I will come with you for I have

as much right as anyone to know what is happening,' I told her, removing my bonnet and all the while wondering what implication the finding of Kieran's first wife had on our marriage.

As we entered the drawing room I could see two men, both strangers and middle-aged standing by the cream settle, their top hats under their arms. Kieran and Derrick sat on the settle facing the door, my husband's face was visibly drained of colour, while his brother looked as calm as always. Both brothers indicated for Justine and I to sit opposite them.

'This is my wife, Barbara,' my husband introduced me to the two strangers, 'and our sister, Justine.'

'How do you do,' said both men in unison.

'Is it true Kieran what our house-keeper has just told us?' asked Justine, looking at her two brothers and the two official looking men for an answer.

'Mr Johnson here will tell you both,' said Kieran in his measured voice, reminding me of our wedding day.

'I'm sorry to tell you ladies, but the body of a young woman was found this morning by a young farmer in his stretch of the river farther down at Nant Peris. As we have only one reported missing person on our list in the area being that of the young Mrs Annabel Alexander, who tragically, so it seems, fell into the river beneath Rowan Falls in early July last year, we are following this line of enquiry first,' explained Mr Johnson admirably, causing me to wonder how Kieran could possibly marry me so soon after this tragic accident.

Getting to my feet and walking over to look out of the window, noting my sampler and the workbox still on the chair I had sat in only this morning when there had been some air of normality in this room.

'I know this must be distressing for you,' said Derrick's voice as he came over to me and placed a gentle hand on my shoulder, but today I was more worried about Kieran. Any other time I would have found solace in Derrick's gesture. 'So what is to happen now?' I asked, walking over to the two men and looking at my husband.

'I'm afraid, Mr Alexander will need to accompany us to the mortuary to identify his wife's body, which will be difficult after a space of six months, but the young woman's clothes should give a clue,' said Mr Johnson, the other stranger remaining silent.

'Can you remember what your wife was wearing on the day of the accident, Mr Alexander?'

'Yes, I can Sir, vividly,' said Kieran, rising from his seat and coming over to my side and placing an arm around my shoulder just as Kerensa Templeton burst through the door. My husband and I both turned our heads to look at her.

'What is amiss?' she said, taking in the scene of Kieran and I close together and I smiled to myself for I felt a victory over her once more. 'Am

I to understand that the downtrodden Annabel has been found?' she said disrespectfully.

At her words Kieran squeezed my shoulder and released me, walking over to Kerensa he said in a menacing voice, 'If you have nothing but insults to bandy about then please leave the room.'

'But darling,' Kerensa began, but Kieran interrupted her once more.

'Derrick, please escort Kerensa from the room. I am in no mood for her today.' As Derrick did as he was bid the lovely young woman cast a disdainful look in my direction and swept out of the room, the skirts of her beautiful pale green dress catching in the door as Derrick went to close it.

'You imbecile!' she berated him and as she disappeared out of the door into the hallway I smiled a secret smile.

'I apologise for that ill-mannered interruption,' apologised my husband, 'now back to where we were,' he continued. 'You asked about Annabel's clothing. If my memory serves me correctly she wore a lilac coloured dress and cloak, the colour which suited her best.'

'Then,' said Mr Johnson, 'if you could accompany us now before the light starts to fade I'd be grateful.'

'I'll come with you,' offered Justine, who had not spoken at all during the conversation.

'No,' I said, stopping her as she made to rise from the settle. 'I shall go, for as Kieran's wife I feel it is my duty.' The first duty I will have performed for him I thought, other than marrying him was my notion and I couldn't understand why I had so willingly offered to go.

As we walked into the hallway and Justine helped me to arrange my bonnet, I could see Kerensa standing next to Derrick, an unbecoming scowl on her face once more. She went to say something but Derrick caught hold of her arm. She almost spat at him as loosening his grip she ran over to Kieran.

'Where are they taking you? Please allow me to come with you, please,' she pleaded, but to no avail as Kieran removed her from him and dramatically she started weeping.

'It's all right, Kerensa,' I told her, 'I shall accompany my husband, for that is what wives do.' At my words she fled over to Derrick and collapsed in his arms. As we went to walk out of the front doors I turned back and noticed Derrick kiss the top of her beautiful head. So, I thought, she is now going to captivate the younger brother.

As we travelled back along the road to Llanberis, Kieran sat next to me, a hand over mine. I wondered if this were to show unity in front of the two officers and I didn't honestly know if I preferred this to be the case or not. I was confused at my feelings, but not so confused as I was to be later that day.

The journey proved to be most uncomfortable, and by the time we reached the small building where the young woman's body lay I was quite nauseous.

I felt some sympathy for my husband as he left me where I sat in a small room to go and identify Annabel's body, if indeed it was she. When he reemerged his face was ashen.

'Was it her?' I asked.

'The clothes were certainly the ones she wore. Oh my God, what have I done?' And he held his head in his hands. 'I've been so foolish.'

'What do you mean, Kieran,' I asked of him, feeling quite perplexed at his words.

'Nothing,' he replied, sitting up straight once more.

'And how has it taken so long for the poor young woman to surface?' I asked of Mr Johnson.

'The body had probably got caught on a bush down river, and with the swelling of the water due to the melting snow I suspect the remains of Mrs Alexander got disentangled and moved farther down stream. We don't suspect foul play so you are free to go, Sir,' he said addressing Kieran.

'There's one more thing Mr Johnson has to say to you,' said my husband quietly, and looking at the officer he said, 'Please proceed and tell Barbara what you told me.'

'Tell me what?' I asked of them, turning my wedding ring round and round on my finger.

'I'm sorry to have to tell you young woman, but as you and Mr Alexander wed before the first Mrs Alexander had been found, that your marriage may be null and void. In other words not legally valid.'

I looked at Kieran whose blue eyes reflected sadness.

5

Kieran and I travelled back in the coach in silence. When we entered the hall of Rowan Castle, Justine came across to us, an anxious look on her face.

'Was it Annabel, brother?' Were her first words.

'It was indeed, now, please organise some tea,' Kieran told her and I felt some sympathy for Justine at Kieran's words for she was obviously upset.

As Justine went off to the kitchen to do as he bid, Kieran turned his attention to me. 'I need to talk to you, Barbara. The morning-room would probably be the best place.'

'I agree, Sir,' I replied following him out of the hall and along the familiar corridor which brought to mind the evening I had seen Kieran with Kerensa in the hall and by the time we entered the morning room I could not contain myself.

'How fortuitous, Sir,' I said facing him, 'that we had not shared a room.'

'Please be calm, Barbara,' he urged me in a soothing tone.

'Calm? How can I possibly remain calm?' I turned on him angrily, my skirts swishing on the carpet beneath me as I spoke. 'Do you have any idea what an impossible situation you have put me in?'

'Let us not be hasty,' was Kieran's reply.

'Hasty!' I exclaimed. 'You were surely the one to be hasty by marrying me when poor Annabel, God rest her soul, had only been gone less than seven months, and now I find that after all you have put me through since I arrived at Rowan Castle, that our union, such as it is, may not be legal.'

'But there is the chance it may be,' Kieran had the audacity to say.

'Well, I for one will be happy if the marriage is null and void,' I told him. 'And I feel the best thing I can do while the weather holds is to leave and go back to Shrewsbury.' As I spoke I made my way past Kieran towards the door, but he stopped me, catching hold of my wrist.

'Stay, please stay, give me a chance to make amends,' he pleaded.

'I think, Sir, that any relationship we may have had is beyond repair, now please release me.'

As I spoke the words, he hesitated before letting me go and as I made to leave the room he said quietly, 'I shall not let this go, madam.'

Leaving the pleasant morning-room and walking back to the hallway with each step I took was a resolve to leave Rowan this very day, but I hadn't bargained on bumping into Justine across the hallway.

'All is not well, Barbara,' she said walking swiftly towards me, 'I perceive it by the expression on your face and the purposeful way you walk. What is wrong?'

'It would appear that the marriage between your brother and myself may be illegal,' I told her, stopping in front of her.

'And what formalities are to be taken to resolve this?' she asked me quietly.

'I have little idea,' I told her, 'but my thought is to leave Rowan Castle today.'

'Surely not!' exclaimed Justine, a shocked look on her lovely face, her blue eyes looking at me with disbelief. 'I will not let you go. In fact, I forbid it until such a time as this matter has been substantiated. It's bad enough that Annabel has been found dead, but for you to leave would be a double setback for the Alexander family and there are your beautiful gowns, being stitched probably at this very moment.'

As Justine spoke the words I realised I had not given our visit to the dressmaker a thought. As we stood together in the hallway Justine placed a gentle hand over mine just as Mrs Burnet came from the direction of the kitchens carrying a large tray, closely followed by Ginny, a plate laden with cakes in her hand.

'Shall we place this in the drawing-room, Miss?' The housekeeper asked Justine as she smiled at me.

'Yes please,' said my sister-in-law, who then turned her attention back to me.

'Come, Barbara,' she persuaded, 'let us talk about this over a nice cup of hot tea.'

As she spoke, Kieran appeared from the direction of the morning-room, looking at both of us he said, 'I have been a fool, yes indeed.' With which words he disappeared up the beautiful staircase.

Justine and I sat drinking tea and talking over the day's events.

'Why would Kieran marry me so soon after the loss of his wife?' I asked her, for this was the question which I kept asking myself.

'Kieran must have loved you and indeed needed companionship,' Justine said.

'But there was no mention of love from either of us. In truth, I adore your brother, so if you ask why did I marry him, I can answer the question,' I told her, and then there was Kerensa. Why had Kieran not married her? So I asked the question and Justine's reply shocked me a little.

'Because,' she began, 'my father left a clause in his will that Kieran and Kerensa should not marry.'

'But why should this be?' I said with curiosity. 'And does Kerensa know of this?'

'As to why, I don't know the answer, but I am sure Kieran does and will not speak of it. Kerensa doesn't know and we have been asked not to tell her.'

'But why not?' I asked with some exasperation, 'for it is plain to see that the young woman adores your brother and he, her.'

'You are right about her, Barbara, she does adore Kieran, but I have my suspicions that Kieran does not feel the same,' she told me, and I wanted so much to tell her of the scene I had witnessed in the hall, but something thankfully stopped me. 'So will you stay?' asked Justine, rising from her seat and walking across to the window.

The light was fading fast and we were talking by firelight which cast soft shadows across the lovely peaceful room. Justine turned back, retracing her steps and came to sit beside me on the settle.

'Please stay,' she said softly, and I was reminded of the very same words Kieran had spoken only an hour since which strangely seemed like a lifetime ago and I set to wondering what his thoughts were at this moment. The shock of identifying Annabel would have been an ordeal for anyone and I suddenly felt uncharitable at the way I had berated him in the morning-room, today of all days.

'You have persuaded me with your kind words,' I agreed, 'on condition that I am moved from the marital bedroom until such time as I have a right to be there.'

'Very well, Barbara, I shall instruct

Mrs Burnet to prepare the yellow room for you,' agreed Justine.

'So we are all happy,' I said as Justine kissed me on the cheek and went over to pull the bell cord to summon Mrs Burnet.

Megan and the housekeeper moved my clothes and meagre belongings to my new room, which was a pleasant enough room with yellow brocade curtains at the windows and around the four-poster bed. A fire was soon burning cheerfully in the small black hearth.

'There, mistress,' said Peggy Burnet, 'I do hope you feel settled in here. It's none of my business why you have moved but we will make you as comfortable as we can, won't we, Megan. Now, you come and sit on this armchair by the fire and try and get some rest,' she said, plumping up a pretty floral cushion to place behind me. Just as I made myself comfortable Kerensa burst unannounced into the room.

'So,' she began, surveying the room as she spoke, 'You've moved, I knew it wouldn't last with Kieran, and now Annabel has been found it will be the end of your reign here,' she told me unkindly, gloating at my predicament.

'Off with you, Miss Kerensa,' said Peggy Burnet, shooing the beautiful girl out of the room, but not before I had looked at her and said in a strong voice, 'This mouse has found wings, Kerensa.' The startled expression on her face made up for all the mixed fortunes this day had brought and I knew that the lovely Kerensa would know I had heard what she had called me and would no doubt flee to Kieran to tell him. Splendid, I thought, for he would know as well as she that I had witnessed the scene in the hall.

That night I lay in bed in my unfamiliar surroundings, the candle-light flickering over the yellow walls and I wondered what was to become of me now.

Next morning after Megan had

drawn back the curtains, I slipped out of bed and stepped across to the window looking out over the scene before me. I could see that I was now situated at the back of the castle for the view was completely different. I could see the stables and a large rose garden surrounded by a low wall which in summer would be a lovely place to sit, but I doubted I would see a summer here, and I mused as to how the validity of my marriage would be ascertained.

I was to learn later that Kieran had it all in hand. As I thought of him he burst into the room just as Kerensa had the previous evening. I was startled at his intrusion for I was not yet dressed and I pulled my robe tightly around me.

'What bad manners,' I berated him.

'Madam, you are, if you remember, my wife,' he said quietly.

'At this moment in time we are not certain of that, remember?' I said cuttingly.

'No matter, I have come to remind

you of your promise to accompany me to Rowan Falls today,' he said.

'I have not forgotten,' I told him, which was a small lie, for it had slipped my mind. 'I will meet you in the hall at 10.30 as we agreed, but I will not ride bareback on your horse as you wished for it is unladylike and I have never ridden a horse before.'

'Very well, Barbara, we will take the pony and trap for it is a pleasant enough February day,' he conceded. 'And Barbara, all will be well, trust me,' were his departing words at which I scoffed, for how could I possibly trust someone who now treated me as a stranger, not a wife.

I wore the wine-coloured velvet once more and thought momentarily how pleased I would be when my new gowns were ready. Mrs Harding, the dress-maker, had said to return in a week's time. Maybe Justine would be kind enough to lend me another gown until then for she and I were the same size and height. Waiting in the hall for

Kieran, his brother came over to me with his usual cheery smile.

'And where are you going, fair damsel?' he asked.

'With Kieran to Rowan Falls,' I answered, blushing at Derrick's words.

'Then be careful that my beloved brother doesn't push you in,' he said, the smile vanishing from his face. His words shocked me.

'Why do you say that?' I questioned.

'No matter, it was a foolish thing to say, enjoy your outing,' Derrick said and I had the briefest feeling as he walked away that he was jealous. What gave me that notion I had little idea but I knew I was right.

Kieran and I settled ourselves in the pony and trap, Kieran wrapping a blanket snugly around my legs for although the sun shone weakly the air was chill and I wondered if we would see any more snow this winter. It was a pleasing ride as we bowled along the country lane, the mountains rising majestically in the distance.

We came to a halt at the beginning of a rough track, Kieran helped me down, his hand lingering in mine and I had a pleasant feeling of being safe, which belied Derrick's words.

'Link your arm through mine, wife,' said Kieran gently, 'for the track is uneven and I don't wish you to twist your pretty ankle.' Kieran's words caused me to realise he was being most charming today and I wondered at his change of heart and also mused as to what the lovely Kerensa would have to say about our outing together.

I heard the pounding of the water before I saw the falls and when they did come into view I gasped at the beauty of it, the water cascading down the high craggy rock was captivating. All we could hear was the rush of water as it tumbled down and over the large rocks in the river below. I stepped nearer to look at the frothy water which caressed the large boulders, and Kieran caught my arm pulling me back and I had an instinctive feeling that this was how Annabel had fallen to her death.

Kieran's face was full of genuine concern and pain and I had at last seen a different side to his character once more in the briefest of moments. We couldn't hear each other speak for the pounding of water, we just stood side by side for some time watching the beauty of the waterfall.

After some time we walked back to the pony and trap, my clothes were slightly damp where the water had sprayed me with a fine mist as it went on its merry way down the gorge but it didn't bother me, I felt content and I realised it was because I had at last shared another pleasant moment with the man I'd married that day in the grim chapel.

'What do you think of my favourite spot?' asked Kieran as we left the roar of the water behind us.

'It is beautiful, I am enraptured by it,' I told him honestly, 'and I wish so much to see it again one day soon.'

'You shall, I promise you. It pleases me that you loved it so much for it is one thing at last we share, the love of Rowan Falls. If only you could learn to love me, too?' he said almost to himself and I turned away as if I hadn't heard, my heart racing and my whole being feeling a contentment I'd never expected to feel.

Arriving back at the castle, Kerensa spoilt the moment, it was almost as if she were waiting for our return.

'Where have you been, Kieran darling?' she gushed, coming over to us and totally ignoring me as if I weren't there, which irked me more than I cared to admit.

'We've been to Rowan Falls,' I told her, my voice angry.

'I hate the place,' she said unexpectedly, 'It's far too noisy and damp for my liking.' She went to put her arms around Kieran's neck, but he pushed her away from him.

'Remove yourself from me, Kerensa,' he told her quite kindly.

'What has happened to you, Kieran?' she said in a rage, stamping her foot and looking at me with hatred in her eyes. 'You've surely not fallen for the mouse!' she screamed, total contempt in her voice.

'These games have got to stop, for games they are,' Kieran told her sharply. 'You are old enough now to have respect for people and thankfully I have just come to realise it. Now, go and find something to do.'

I was amazed at Kieran's words, had their closeness just been some game he indulged in to please her? Even if this was the case, he had failed to see that the young woman was besotted by him.

'I have a new sampler you can stitch,' I offered her kindly.

'Sampler! You can keep your sampler. I have no time for ladies' mundane pursuits, far better to be out riding a horse with the wind in your hair,' she said to me with some disdain. Then she looked back at Kieran, 'And you, sir, will tire of this woman for she has no fire in her blood.' With which words she flounced off in the direction of the drawing-room where a moment later we heard the sound of the piano being played with gusto.

'I apologise for Kerensa's rudeness. I will not let her be rude to you again, she may have the fire in her blood but you are a gentlewoman and deserve better,' he assured me.

As Kieran left me to keep an appointment in Llanberis, which I assumed to be pertaining to Annabel, I made my way to the ballroom for I wished to see the picture of Rowan Falls once more. As I entered the vast room I looked around me, imagining people in vibrant-coloured clothes whirling around the floor in celebration and me in my beautiful shimmering turquoise gown and my husband captivated by it.

But these were daydreams and would no doubt never take place now. I had a strong feeling that my marriage was indeed a sham and yet I had today once more seen the better side of the man I had married.

As I lay in bed that night thinking of our visit to the waterfall, I felt that a warm glow surrounded me. I could hear the crackle of the fire as it burned low in the hearth and hear my heart beating at the thought of my husband, who indeed may not be my husband, and I resolved to set the wheels in motion tomorrow to find out for certain for I needed to know.

As these thoughts warmed me and I was about to fall asleep I imagined I heard the sound of someone sobbing. I listened again and realised I had not imagined it, somewhere close by a woman was sobbing. Swiftly I got out of bed, it seemed to be coming from the chimney breast. Was it Kerensa?

I wondered as I listened to the painful sound, but it could not be her for her room I had learned was at the other end of the corridor. Then who was it? The sound subsided and I got back into bed listening for some time, but the sound didn't come again and I drifted into a peaceful slumber resolving to ask Mrs Burnet who slept on the other side of the chimney.

6

Next morning after Megan had helped me prepare for breakfast in my grey day dress she went in search of Mrs Burnet for me. Half-an-hour later the house-keeper appeared in my room, the keys jangling at her waist.

'Megan said you wished to see me, mistress,' she said.

'Can you tell me, Mrs Burnet, who sleeps in the room the other side of my chimney breast?' I asked her.

This morning after thinking it over I was more perplexed than ever as I'd been to Justine's room so I knew it wasn't her, so if it wasn't Justine or Kerensa, who else could it be? Apart from myself they were the only females in the castle excluding the servants, and surely it couldn't possibly be one of them, I waited with some anticipation for the housekeeper's reply.

'It's the uninhabited wing of the castle, mistress,' she told me looking somewhat perplexed herself. 'No-one sleeps there to my knowledge, why do you ask?'

At Peggy Burnet's question I hesitated as to whether to tell her but decided I could trust her. 'I heard the sound of weeping and it appeared to be coming from behind the chimney.'

'That's strange, mistress.' And at her words I was waiting for her to ask me if I'd imagined it, but she didn't.

'Have you any idea whose room it is the other side of the chimney?' I asked.

'Well I think it was the mistress' room,' offered Peggy Burnet.

'You mean my husband's first wife?' I said feeling more perplexed than ever.

'Bless me, no,' was her reply, ''t'was the old master's wife who slept in that room, the first mistress Annabel.'

'And have you the key to this room?' I then asked.

'I have, mistress, but no-one is to go

there,' the housekeeper said with some alarm.

'You agree that I am the mistress here?' I asked gently.

'I do indeed,' she replied adamantly.

'Then please give me the key. If any one challenges you then it is my fault,' I instructed her.

'Very well,' she agreed, 'but I must accompany you, you will never find it with all these corridors being like a maze,' the housekeeper said kindly.

'I'll meet you back here after breakfast if you are agreeable, shall we say ten o'clock?' I suggested.

'That suits me fine, mistress. I can get on with my other tasks in the meantime,' Peggy agreed.

'And please Peggy, tell no-one,' I told her as she left the room.

'Don't worry, mistress. I can keep my mouth closed,' the housekeeper assured me and I did indeed trust her.

Entering the dining room I could see that Kerensa was there in earnest conversation with Derrick, they both stopped talking when they saw me.

'Please don't let me interrupt your conversation,' I told them as I served myself some breakfast and then seating myself opposite Derrick I helped myself to coffee. Kerensa wore the colour green today once more, which suited her admirably, matching her startling green eyes.

'And where is your husband?' she asked almost civilly, but I detected the hint of sarcasm in her petulant voice.

'I have no idea,' I answered, wishing that I had so that I could surprise her with my answer.

'He could be anywhere on the estate,' offered Derrick smiling at me. 'It's a sad business about Annabel,' he observed, not looking at me as he spoke, but down at his plate.

'Yes it is,' I said quietly, 'but it was to be expected.'

'What would you know about what is to be expected in this household?'

Kerensa turned on me. 'You are an intruder just as Annabel was.' At her words I noticed that today, Derrick did not jump to my defence.

'I am not an intruder and nor was poor Annabel,' I retorted, 'I am Kieran's wife whether you like it or not.'

'But Kieran loves me,' she simpered.

'To be honest Kerensa, I don't think that Kieran has ever loved anyone,' and as I made my way back to my room after this unfortunate encounter I realised that I was probably right. My husband had never loved and found it difficult to do so. Yes, I thought, I am right and I fervently hoped that my husband was starting to fall in love with me.

Mrs Burnet was waiting for me as promised and she led me through a couple of unfamiliar corridors until we stopped outside an oak door in what was obviously a neglected part of the castle.

As we entered the room both the housekeeper and I stood on the threshold and looked at each other with amazement.

The pretty room was for all intents and purposes still occupied, a fire even burned in a small white marble fireplace. We both stepped farther into the room.

'Well!' exclaimed Mrs Burnet. 'This I cannot explain, for believe me when I say that I knew nothing about it, and I'm certain that the servant girls don't either. It's a real mystery to be sure.'

The room was cosy and warm with peach-coloured finishings. There was no four-poster bed here, but a charming brass bed head and bed end with a colourful hand-stitched quilt which covered what appeared to be a feather mattress, a snowy white bolster peeping out from beneath.

A beautiful porcelain clock decorated with peach roses stood on the mantel and showed the time as 10.30 which was correct I thought as I looked at the fob watch pinned to my dress. A scent of roses hung in the air and going over to the dressing table I picked up a crystal glass perfume bottle which did indeed contain the perfume, someone had obviously sprayed it recently. Under the window was a towel rail on which were folded towels of peach and white.

'They are from the laundry room and still smell fresh,' Mrs Burnet exclaimed picking one up and placing it under her nose. 'I cannot explain this, it is almost as if someone was living here. Wait 'til I tell my David.'

'No, Mrs Burnet,' I cautioned her. 'Please tell no-one, not even your husband.'

'Very well, mistress,' she agreed, 'but how are we to solve the mystery? And you heard sobbing you say?'

'Yes I did and it will be interesting to see if it happens again tonight,' I said going over to the window. Although we had come down different corridors to this room, the view was the same as mine, only nearer to the rose garden. If this were the first Annabel's room then I had the distinct feeling she loved roses.

I was loathe to leave this room for the atmosphere was calm and serene but I knew that I must in case the occupant returned unexpectedly, if indeed there was an occupant or was someone keeping Annabel's memory alive.

That night as I lay in bed mulling over this mystery the sobbing started once more, I looked at the small clock on the table by my bed and I could see it was the hour of midnight.

Putting on my robe I quietly opened my bedroom door and looked down the corridor, I could see there was no one about, and no sign of life at all so I made my way to Annabel's room, praying I was going in the right direction as one corridor looked very much like another with the carpeting underfoot the same.

Just as I was nearing the neglected corridor Derrick stepped out of a room and it was impossible for me to hide, in any case he had already seen me, he looked somewhat shocked to see me but smiled nonetheless coming towards me.

'Well, well Barbara,' he exclaimed, 'I had not expected you to be wandering around the castle at this time of night in your night attire and with bare feet,' he said looking down at my feet which were indeed bare, causing me to blush and not knowing what reason I was going to give for me wandering the castle after midnight.

'I appear to have lost my way,' I said quickly.

'Then it is fortunate I was stepping out of my room,' Derrick said. 'I will escort you back.' At these words I said a silent oath for now I would not be able to ascertain if the sobbing were indeed coming from Annabel's lovely room. As Derrick escorted me back the way I had come, his hand on my elbow, I prayed we would not meet a soul for it would appear to anyone that I was in a compromising position with my husband's brother. Thankfully we met no-one and as I stood with Derrick outside my bedroom door bidding him goodnight he took me in his arms.

'What are you doing?' I exclaimed.

'I have really taken to you Barbara, and just wish to hold you. If your marriage to Kieran proves to be unlawful then please marry me. I promise I will treat you with the respect you deserve, unlike the way my brother treats you.'

I was shocked at his words for I had not seen it coming, except that the day I had visited the falls with Kieran I had thought Derrick to be jealous and it would now appear my instinct was right. Just as Derrick bent towards me to kiss me I managed to wriggle free.

'How dare you, Sir! We will speak no more of this,' I told him angrily, 'I bid you goodnight.'

'You will see that I am better for you than my brother ever will be,' were his words as I closed the door on him wishing I could lock it. I leant against the door for some time hoping that he wouldn't trouble me again and after a short while I heard his footsteps walking down the corridor.

I breathed a sigh of relief and got back into bed, but my sleep that night was a restless one and I wondered if Derrick's proposal had been genuine, but I assured myself that I would not put myself in that situation again with my husband's brother no matter what a charming person he was.

A week passed after the incident, I saw Derrick several times when he was his usual self and I began to imagine that the unfortunate incident had been a figment of my imagination. Kieran was charming and kept his distance from Kerensa much to her chagrin, but I saw little of my husband and we were no nearer to finding out if our marriage were indeed legal but that was all to change very soon, the sobbing had ceased also for a week.

It was today that Justine and I were to travel back to Mrs Harding. the dressmaker, We decided to take the carriage as although nearing the end of February the cloudy skies were laden with rain, but thankfully the snow had not returned to keep us indoors.

I was very excited about our outing and anxious to see what Mrs Harding had done with the materials I'd chosen.

'Come in,' she said as she met us at the door. She took us to a large room at the back of the house where there were three tailors' dummies. On one hung my beautiful ball gown.

'How enchanting!' I enthused, going over to it and running the pale turquoise silk through my fingers. I'd never seen a dress as exquisite as this let alone having one belong to me. 'Can I try it on first?' I asked like an anxious child wishing to play with a new toy.

'Let us see the other gowns first,' suggested Justine. 'It is far better to save the best until last.'

'I've made you four day dresses and two evening gowns,' Mrs Harding told me. 'I'll just get my seamstress, Polly, to help me bring them in.'

While Mrs Harding was gone I went back over once more to the gown, marvelling at how the three roses at the neckline looked so real.

'You are really taken with that gown, aren't you,' said Justine indulgently just as Mrs Harding returned with Polly and a couple of my dresses. Trying them on I marvelled that the dressmaker had got everything right from the size to the length. I looked at my reflection in the mirror at the lilac dress I was wearing, the neckline and wrists edged with cream lace and just as I had felt wearing the wine-coloured velvet I could hardly believe it was me.

It was the same with the other gowns in pinks and blues, I was overwhelmed by it all and by the time I tried my ballgown on I was almost in tears, realising my good fortune and I knew that I had Kieran to thank for marrying me a few weeks ago. How I prayed that things would work out between us for we had certainly reached a tacit understanding during the past week.

Polly and Mrs Harding slipped the ball gown over my head and it fell into place with little arranging, the turquoise silk shimmered in the daylight and I bent down to pick up the hem allowing me to admire the small turquoise flowers which had been stitched perfectly to it.

'You look beautiful, Barbara, my brother will not be able to resist you when he sees you, and I suggest a long pair of white gloves will finish the effect admirably. Don't you agree, Mrs Harding?' She looked to the dressmaker for advice.

'I agree totally,' she said.

'Would you like to wear one of your new gowns for our return to the castle?' Justine asked.

'Could I?' I asked, not having thought it.

'Of course you can,' laughed Justine.

Reluctantly I let them remove the ball gown, the soft silk feeling luxurious on my skin. I selected a cornflower blue gown to wear back to the castle, it had a high necked pointed bodice with full skirts and lace of perfect blue stitched at the neckline.

As we left Mrs Harding's I felt a different woman, my experiences since I had arrived at Rowan Castle had transformed me from a quiet, shy, retiring young woman into a self-assured one.

'Mistress!' exclaimed Megan as I stepped into my room. 'You look right beautiful and the colour suits you perfectly.'

'Thank you,' I replied enjoying the compliment. Megan was replenishing the fire and as she got to her feet she asked where the other gowns were. 'They are following later,' I told her.

'I can't wait to see them, truly I can't,' she said excitedly. 'The master was looking for you earlier,' she then told me. 'I told him you'd be back mid-afternoon. I hope I did the right thing.'

'Absolutely the right thing,' I assured her. When she left I sat on the armchair by the fire arranging my lovely skirts around me and musing over what Kieran wanted to seek me out for and I was soon to find out for no sooner had I thought it than he knocked on the door and entered quietly. For some time he stood there looking at me before he spoke.

'You look charming, Barbara,' he said at last. 'I hope that you will wear it often.'

'If it pleases you, Sir I shall,' I told him, hot colour suddenly suffusing my cheeks.

'I would be most pleased if you would after all these weeks call me by my Christian name again,' he said thoughtfully.

'Kieran,' I said out loud, letting the name fall from my lips like a caress.

'It is so easy, isn't it?' he said laughing and I realised that he was right, I had used his name before, but not since our arrival at the castle. This surely was a step forward.

'Are you comfortable in here, Barbara?' he enquired, his eyes dancing around the room, his gaze resting momentarily on the bed.

'I am very comfortable,' I assured him.

'There was no need for you to vacate the marital bedroom,' he said and without preamble pulled a high-backed chair opposite me by the fire.

'I'm sorry to say that there was, and it was on that condition that I didn't leave Rowan the day poor Annabel was found. Did you love her? Annabel I mean.'

'I realise now that I never did,' he told me honestly, so my assumption had been right.

'And what of Kerensa?' I had to ask and he paused for some seconds before answering.

'I have no love for Kerensa either,' his words astonished me after the moments I had seen them together in the past weeks.

'What do you feel for her?' I asked quietly.

'Compassion,' was his simple answer.

'And why is that?' I asked him gently.

'Because she loves me and I cannot

return it. She is but a child still and vents her feelings on both me and Derrick. I play games with her to keep her amused and sane,' he told me.

'Are you saying she loves Derrick also?' I asked softly.

'Yes indeed she does, but my brother will not indulge in her games, he is too serious about everything,' he answered.

'And here was me thinking that Derrick was the humorous one and you the serious one,' I said laughing.

'Beware Barbara, for first impressions can often be deceiving and lead you into danger. Beware of my brother for he is a wolf in sheep's clothing.' Kieran was serious as he spoke and I thought back to the incident in the corridor a few days ago, but I would not tell my husband for fear of causing trouble.

'I will heed your warning, husband,' I said, praying all the while that he was indeed my legal spouse.

'Do you like it here at Rowan Castle?' he asked unexpectedly.

'I love it and can't wait for the spring

to arrive so we can go walking in the gardens,' I began, secretly wondering at the same time if this would ever be possible.

'Your dream sounds idyllic. I must apologise for the way I have treated you since our marriage, I am very unhappy about the way Annabel ended her life, but let us talk no more of it for now at least. I sought you out to tell you something.' Here he paused and lent forward in the chair, his hands hanging loosely between his knees and his head bowed, then he lifted his head and looked me in the eye before continuing. 'The hearing regarding our marriage is to be held tomorrow. We are both to attend.'

'And what time is this?' I asked him and I realised that the time of reckoning was nigh.

'Not until two pm. I apologise that you are to be put through this ordeal, but due to my own stupidity I have brought this situation about for which I apologise profusely.'

'I accept your apology, Kieran. We shall face it together,' I assured him, for I could see he was repentant. As Kieran left me he looked back as he stood by the open door and said, 'I shall pray tonight for our future, little one.'

As I lay in bed that night the sobbing started again, but to solve that mystery I would have to wait until after tomorrow and I too silently prayed that all would be well for my husband and I; for I realised even more how much I loved and adored him, and I knew in my heart nothing would change it.

7

After breakfast the next morning there was great excitement when my gowns arrived from the dressmakers. Megan was waiting for me when I came out of the dining-room.

'Your dresses have arrived, mistress,' she told me and I walked up the staircase with her as anxious as she to see them. When we entered my room I could see they had been laid across my bed in a profusion of colour, walking across I looked at them hardly believing they now belonged to me.

'We had best hang them in the wardrobe, Megan,' I told her my voice aquiver.

'Aren't you going to try one on, mistress?' Megan said with disappointment in her voice.

'Of course I will,' I agreed, picking up the beautiful turquoise silk ballgown.

'Let us hang this first for it is special,' I said, all the while wondering if I would ever have cause to wear it, which brought to mind the hearing this very day. Megan and I were laughing while I stood in a pale lemon gown with a high neck and long sleeves, the lace of which fell over the back of my hand.

'You look lovely, mistress,' said Megan walking around me admiring the fullness of the skirts.

'I agree,' said Kieran's voice from the doorway. Megan and I had been so distracted by the beautiful gowns that we had not heard the door open.

'I'll leave you, mistress,' said Megan as she looked at the master, so saying she gave a brief curtsey to Kieran and scuttled from the room closing the door behind her.

Kieran stepped farther towards me, surveying me as he did so, 'I've come to ask if you'll walk with me around the outside of the castle,' he began, 'for it is a pleasant enough day for late February.'

'I would like that very much, but I shall need to change my gown,' I told him.

'No, please stay as you are for you look exquisite.' And I realised that my hair was escaping its pins, so swiftly I went over to the dressing table and rearranged it as best I could with trembling hands. This was indeed a surprise and a very pleasant one that Kieran should seek me out.

'I'll need my shawl,' I told him, searching through the chest of drawers. I found it easy enough as there was very little in there. 'I am ready.' I told him and so it was that Kieran and I walked down the main staircase of Rowan Castle together for the first time. I felt proud and elated as Mrs Burnet crossed the hall.

'Good morning, master, good morning, mistress,' she greeted us as she went about her business and then Kerensa crossed the hall in front of us dressed in a lovely beige-coloured riding outfit.

'And where are you two going together?' she asked rudely.

'It is hardly your business, young woman,' said Kieran light-heartedly, 'but we are going for a walk.'

'You'd be more suited to come riding with me. I intend to ride out to the beach at Abermenai Point with Derrick, I can't imagine what has happened to you, unless you are in love?' As she spoke she threw me an indignant glance.

'Play your games somewhere else, Kerensa,' Kieran said dismissing the fact she was there completely and taking hold of my arm in his.

'How could you dismiss me so easily after all the years I have loved you?' she wailed. 'You have no idea how much I care for you, she'll never love you like I do.'

'I'm sorry you feel this way, but I cannot return that love, we are more like sister and brother, this is what I feel for you, a brotherly devotion.' As Kieran spoke the words I thought of the night I had seen Kerensa sat on Kieran's bed. Had I dreamt it I mused, and the whole conversation had spoilt the joy of Kieran seeking me out to walk with me. We left Kerensa weeping in Derrick's arms and as Kieran and I walked across the front of the castle I felt I had to be honest with him.

'Kieran,' I began, stopping at the same time and looking directly at his handsome face, 'I have a confession to make.' Here I hesitated, was I doing the right thing?

'Confess then pretty lady,' he said urging me to speak.

'A short while after my arrival here I went to the door of your room to speak with you, the door was ajar and I could see Kerensa standing next to your bed, framed by the moonlight,' here I paused, 'which leads me to believe she has a great love for you.' There, I'd said it, but what would be my husband's reply? What he did say startled me somewhat.

'I can honestly say, Barbara, that I

have never loved Kerensa, but whatever she feels for me I have no control over it. As much as I have told her I cannot love her, she pursues me. I am at a loss to what course of action to take next. Do you believe me, little one?' Kieran asked earnestly.

'Yes I do,' I told him honestly just as Derrick and Kerensa rode past us on their mounts, hers a lovely grey and Derrick's a horse as black as thunder. He doffed his hat as he passed and I realised I didn't know what to make of Kieran's younger brother and wondered if I should tell Kieran about the incident in the corridor.

'Can we continue our walk now, madam?' Kieran asked as we both watched Derrick and Kerensa disappear out of sight down the driveway. 'Or have you another confession to make?' he said, his blue eyes twinkling.

'Yes, I have,' I told him and he laughed.

'Then let us walk while you recount it or we shall both be too cold to carry on.' So we walked and I told of the evening I had seen him with Kerensa in the hallway.

'So why do you do these things? Have you such little respect for me?' Here Kieran stopped.

'I will answer that question after we have walked around the castle, for then I wish to show you something and explain it to you,' he told me, so we continued our walk, he pointing out the marital bedroom to me and as we rounded the corner to the back of the castle he showed me the stables and introduced me to his horse, Lancelot.

'A true knight,' said Kieran laughing as I backed away from the overbearing presence of the great beast. 'He will not harm you.' and he called to David, the housekeeper's husband, to bring a lump or two of sugar. 'Now hold this in the palm of your hand and offer it to Lancelot,' he instructed. The sugar lumps lay in my palm and slowly I moved my hand towards the horse's mouth.

Lancelot was surprisingly gentle as he bent his head and took the sugar, his wet nose tickling the palm of my hand, I laughed.

'There Barbara, you and he are friends already,' said Kieran with mirth in his voice, for I must have looked petrified.

We carried on to the rear of the rose garden, the rose bushes had been pruned and appeared to be sitting waiting to flower and for the summer sun. My husband pointed out my bedroom high up in the wall.

'The apartments next to you are unoccupied. It's where my parents slept and where the nurseries are.' As he spoke I wondered if I should confess that I had visited his mother's room, but something stopped me from doing so for I felt it would upset him. We were at the far end of the castle now and I could see a delightful terrace which in the afternoon would face the sun.

Kieran led me up a couple of wide steps and we stepped on to the flag stones beneath our feet. It was like being perched on an island with a glorious view over the rose garden.

'And here,' said Kieran drawing me over to a large window, 'is the ballroom.' As I looked through the window and along to the others I could see that it was indeed the ballroom.

'How perfect!' I enthused for I could imagine attending a ball on a warm summer's evening and coming out through the french windows to stand and look out over a riot of colour in the rose garden. Once more I thought how fortunate I was, which brought to mind our attendance at today's hearing at Llanberis.

'No sad thoughts now, Barbara,' Kieran chided me, 'For I can see that something has caused the smile on your face to fade.' Here he took me in his arms and looking down at me said, 'Whatever the outcome of my foolishness is today, I promise that all will be well.' Here he let me go when I had so longed for him to kiss me, but maybe he thought the time wasn't right. 'Now let us go back indoors for I promised to explain something to you.'

The french windows were unlocked and we walked arm in arm across the ballroom floor, standing together we looked at the picture of Rowan Falls.

'It is beautiful.' I uttered to myself more than to Kieran which caused him to look down at my face.

'You don't know how much it means to me that you love it, for I have loved it since I was a boy. The whole place has such natural beauty and I love the thunder of the water which rings in my ears long after I have left there, serving to remind me of its power.

'And then it has many moods, in the summer when there is little rain the water cascades down in but a trickle compared to the thunder it emits after the rain and snow. You will see it in its many changing moods I promise you,' Kieran assured me and for the second time in his company I felt safe as I had done when we visited the waterfall.

'I do hope so,' I murmured, 'for I can almost imagine that we are there by the way you describe it.'

'Now let us proceed to the lower floor where I have something to show you,' he said steering me from the ballroom and down some steps which I had not noticed before. Suddenly we stepped into a dark panelled room, quite a small room and dark until Kieran lit a lamp which threw its light on a wall facing us where there hung a large portrait of a lovely young woman.

'Who is it?' I asked softly. Her white gown with flowers at the low neckline could almost be the fashion of the today. Blue eyes looked down at me, and the plump red lips were parted in a half smile. I was mesmerised by her beauty, I looked at Kieran for an answer.

'It is my mother, painted when she first came to Rowan Castle as a bride over thirty years ago,' Kieran told me and I could sense the emotion in his voice as he spoke the words.

'And what happened to her?' I asked gently.

'To be honest, Barbara, I do not know for she didn't die here. One moment she was here when I was ten years old and then she was gone and we've not seen her since. I've tried to find her, but in spite of lengthy investigations around the country I have never managed to locate her. She could be dead, but it is the not knowing which grieves me for I truly love her,' he said and I laid a hand gently on his arm.

'So what is it that you wanted to explain?' I asked, for the portrait did not answer my questions.

'I want to explain that when I married poor Annabel I thought I was in love with her, but since I met you I realise now what true love is. I married you because I didn't want to lose you. I loved you from the first moment I set eyes on you in the library. But I suspected that being back at Rowan Castle I would feel a sense of guilt over

Annabel, and I have.

'But my love for you has not diminished, in truth it's grown since we came here, and I longed to tell you. The truth is I should have laid Annabel to rest before I married you. But I was so afraid I'd lose you, my only true love. Do you understand, dear heart?' he said, pulling me into his arms.

Tears welled up in my eyes and we stood for many minutes in a loving embrace, with the first Annabel looking down on us. When we tore ourselves apart he took my face in his hands. 'But now, I am praying that our marriage is legal for I have great respect for you, you have said what you feel and I admire you for that.'

Here he paused again. 'The day you first came with the family to the chapel, I looked at you as you stepped into the hall looking every inch a lady as my mother would have done, and then that very same evening you played the piano so perfectly, you were as one with the chords. I was entranced, captivated and desperately in love all at once.

'A feeling I'd never experienced until I met you, so I failed to understand it until our visit to Rowan Falls, and now if our marriage doesn't exist, I shall find a way to woo you, so you will love me as much as I love you for I want to keep you here to love you and protect you as I should have from the beginning.

'But maybe this was all meant to be, to make me realise my folly.' He stopped, obviously exhausted from the emotion he had put into this declaration.

'I . . . ' I began, but he interrupted me, placing his finger on my lips.

'Let us say no more until after the hearing, let us see what the outcome is and what course we will need to take for I fear it may not go well.'

After lunch, while Megan helped prepare me for our visit to Llanberis, I mulled over all Kieran had told me. It had certainly been a morning full of confessions and had brought me to a greater understanding of the man I had married.

He seemed intent on doing the right thing and I admired him for his honesty, and the fact that he had told me that he loved me pleased my whole being for I knew without any doubt that this was the truth. Now we had to face some stranger who would decide whether we were truly man and wife.

I looked at my reflection in the full length mirror on my wardrobe which contained my beautiful new clothes.

The royal blue velvet suit with the fitted bodice to the neck and the full skirts with a small train suiting the austere occasion admirably. As I put my black gloves on and Megan helped me into my royal blue bonnet with a black band around the brim on my head she said to me, 'I don't know what errand you are on, mistress, but whatever it is I can tell it's a right sombre occasion. I want you to know that I am proud to be your maid and look after you. You are a kind mistress and I,' here Megan broke down in tears and I placed an arm around her, 'and I hope, mistress, that nothing changes.'

'Nothing will change I assure you, Megan.' And as I left her tidying my room I silently prayed that I had told her the truth.

Kieran and I were silent all the way to Llanberis in the carriage, as he helped me down into the street he placed my arms through his and patting my hand smiled down at me. Not a word was spoken, but I knew that today, whatever the outcome we were united at last.

We sat together in a gloomy room side by side on uncomfortable hard-backed chairs, facing a table at which an elderly magistrate sat whom we understood to be a Mr Simmonds. He had no humour in his eyes and scrutinised us both silently before speaking.

My heart was pounding and when I glanced at Kieran who still held on to my arm, I could see his mouth was set in a determined line.

'I have the facts before me, Mr Alexander and Miss Thorpe?' he questioned and I nodded foolishly in reply as if a cat had got my tongue. 'The first Mrs Alexander fell tragically to her death, I understand,' Mr Simmonds said looking at Kieran for an answer.

'Yes indeed,' said Kieran in his measured tone.

'And before her body was recovered you married the lady now sitting at your side?' Mr Simmonds questioned again and I wished with all my heart he would just get on with it.

'That is correct, Sir,' said Kieran politely, which must have pleased the old gentleman.

'Did you not realise that a decree of presumption would be required before you married again?' asked Mr Simmonds.

'No, I did not,' said Kieran.

'Well I have to tell you that exhaustive enquiries should have been made before a second marriage took place. I declare therefore that no valid marriage exists between you and Barbara Thorpe and I declare that you're marriage to Barbara Thorpe is null and void,' Mr Simmonds uttered the words with a flourish and Kieran and I looked at each other with disbelief.

'But I can tell you,' continued Mr Simmonds, 'that now the first Mrs Alexander has been found and identified you are now free to marry, and with all the evidence I have before me there will be no charges brought against either of you. You are therefore free to go.'

As we stepped out into the street once more I burst into tears and Kieran gathered me in his arms once more.

'Marry me, Miss Thorpe?' he said most unexpectedly, 'And this time we will do it properly, little one.' At his words my heart was singing and I wrapped my arms around his neck.

'Yes.' I whispered. 'I will marry you.'

And Kieran bent to kiss me without any thought for where we were and I had no care either as at last his lips met mine with the gentlest of kisses.

8

It's strange how indifference can turn to love, and despair to joy in such a short space of time, but for Kieran and I thankfully it had; and we arrived back at Rowan Castle longing to tell everyone our wedding plans. As we stepped into the hall Mrs Burnet was laying a letter on a silver salver which stood on a table by the main door, seeing us arrive back the letter was forgotten.

'Master, mistress!' she exclaimed, 'I'll be making you both a nice cup of tea,' she said bustling over to us.

'That would be perfect, Mrs Burnet,' Kieran said kindly, 'but what I would like you to do is fetch Justine, Derrick and Kerensa from wherever they may be and ask them to join us in the drawing-room,' he instructed.

'Well I know Master Derrick and

Miss Kerensa have just returned from their ride, but I shall need to locate Miss Justine. I'll get on to it straight away,' said Peggy Burnet going in the direction of the kitchens.

Kieran and I went into the drawing-room when I removed my bonnet and gloves, then we sat together on the cream settle facing the door. Kieran turned me to him.

'Do you agree that we should marry in the chapel here at the end of August? For we must wait a few months, out of respect for Annabel,' he told me softly.

'I agree, and it will give us enough time to arrange everything,' I said, thinking of all that was to be done and the most important thing of all was my wedding dress.

'Six months will be ample enough time, little one. I admit I can hardly wait,' Kieran confessed.

'Shall we pick a date so we can tell the others when they arrive?' I said smiling with happiness. I was longing to tell Justine for I knew she would be happy for us, but I wasn't too sure how Derrick and Kerensa would take the news even though their thought was that we were married already.

'Shall we say the twenty-eighth of August which is about six months away?' suggested Kieran.

'Very well,' I agreed. Just then Justine and Derrick arrived.

'Now let us all be seated for we have something to tell you, haven't we, Barbara,' Kieren said.

Derrick and Justine sat on one settle and Kieran and I on the other opposite them.

'So what have you to tell us?' Justine asked curiously.

'I'd rather wait until Kerensa were here also.' As he spoke Miss Templeton burst through the door, she had changed and now wore the green silk she'd worn on the day of my arrival, the emerald colour matched her eyes perfectly.

'So why have we been summoned? No doubt it's to tell us the marriage is over,' she said sarcastically. Looking at her I could see no resemblance to the other three siblings.

'Sit here Kerensa,' offered Derrick, rising from his seat and sitting on a high-backed chair. Kerensa did as she was bid.

'Well,' she said, 'let us get it over with for I have things to do.'

'It's a rare occasion when you have anything to do except to be rude to others, which is to stop,' Kieran said severely. 'Barbara and I have been to a hearing today regarding the validity of our marriage, and we have to tell you that it has been deemed null and void.'

'What did I tell you!' gloated Kerensa as she stood up and clapped her hands together with glee. 'Now perhaps the little mouse will go back to her hole so we can get back to some normality.' At her words Kieran's face held a look of thunder.

'Sit down!' He shouted at her. 'For I haven't finished, and what I am about to say, young woman will hopefully wipe that smug expression off your face.'

'Let me tell them, Kieran?' I asked quietly, for at this moment I would like nothing better than to upset the gloating Kerensa.

'Your brother, Kieran, and I are engaged to be married, and will marry here at Rowan Chapel on the twenty-eighth of August, giving time for respect for Annabel,' I told them.

'Oh Barbara, Kieran!' said Justine jumping up and coming across to both of us and kissing our cheeks. 'So we can at last attend a wedding, what a happy day this is. We must get to see Mrs Harding at our earliest convenience,' she said excitedly taking both my hands in hers. 'For you will need a wedding dress and I a new outfit. Oh what a happy day! I'll ring for Mrs Burnet to ask David to fetch us a bottle of champagne from the cellar.' With which words she released me and went to pull the bell rope by the fireplace.

'And where's the ring? The Alexander

ring?' asked Kerensa. In all the excitement of our announcement I had almost forgotten her. She had said the words quietly and with menace in her voice and now she looked at Kieran for an answer.

'It is here,' said Kieran softly, as he spoke he drew a small blue velvet box from his pocket. 'Come to me, Barbara,' he said and I went back to the settle where he still sat and he indicated for me to sit where he was; and quite unexpectedly he knelt before me.

My cheeks grew hot as all eyes were on us just as Mrs Burnet answered the call of the bell but the master took little notice. He opened the box and I gasped, for inside nestling amongst the velvet was a glistening round sapphire ring surrounded by diamonds. Kieran took it from the box and taking my hand placed the Alexander ring on my finger. 'We are now officially betrothed before everyone,' he said, rising once more to his feet.

I looked across his shoulder at Mrs

Burnet who hovered in the doorway, a tear in her eyes and out came her hanky once more.

Kerensa however was not smiling at the scene she'd just witnessed and for once she seemed lost for words, but found her voice once more just as I'd thought it.

'You!' she screamed at Kieran, her skirts swishing on the carpet as she turned to my betrothed, her finger pointing at him in a menacing manner, 'You Sir, have broken my heart and I put a curse on both of you. Come Derrick, we will leave them to their ill-timed celebrations.' With which words she flounced out of the room with Derrick at her heels pushing a startled Mrs Burnet to one side as she went.

'Well, I never did in my life before!' exclaimed the housekeeper,. 'May I say congratulations to you master and your lovely lady from my David and me and all you staff here at Rowan. Now you called me,' she said.

'Yes,' said Justine, 'would you be kind enough to ask David to fetch a bottle of champagne from the cellar.'

'I'll do that right away, Miss,' agreed Peggy.

'And Mrs Burnet,' Kieran called her back, 'please tell no-one about the scene you've just witnessed with Miss Kerensa.'

'I won't, I promise, Sir,' she said placing a finger to her lips.

'Take no heed of Kerensa,' soothed Justine when the housekeeper had left us, 'she is fickle that one and as we speak will be casting her spell on Derrick.' As Justine spoke the words I fervently prayed that this would be the case but I had my doubts.

Although I'd drunk champagne I found it very difficult to sleep that night, the mixed events of the day going round and round in my head. Kieran's mother's portrait, being married and then not being married, the engagement ring and Kerensa's outburst all whirling in my mind and I came to the conclusion it was Kerensa's reaction which disturbed me most of all. In all my darkest imaginings I could not have perceived what the outcome would be.

When morning came I had dismissed Kerensa from my mind for Justine and I were to visit Mrs Harding today and I was jubilant at the prospect of our outing.

'I hear congratulations are in order mistress, no I mean Miss,' said Megan, 'I'm real pleased that all is well for I'd have been right sad if you'd had to leave.'

'Well, I'm not, so all is well Megan and today I am to choose the material for my wedding dress,' I told her.

'Oh Miss, it must be the most exciting time for you, but didn't you wear a special dress the first time?' she queried, obviously quite perplexed at the whole situation, which I could well understand.

'No Megan, but this time I intend to choose exactly what I imagine I should wear at my wedding.'

'How lovely, Miss. I look forward to seeing you in your wedding gown,' she said sincerely.

I met Justine in the hall at ten as arranged last evening, I was dressed in the cornflower blue as Kieran had liked it so much, and was so glad I had as he came into the hall just as we were leaving and kissing my hand he whispered, 'Choose well, little one.'

'I think I ought to tell you that Annabel's funeral is to be held next week,' said Justine as we travelled to Llanberis in the carriage. At her words my hand flew to my mouth for I had to confess I had quite forgotten poor Annabel and suddenly I felt that I shouldn't be so happy or making plans for our wedding under these circumstances.

'I can guess what you are thinking, Barbara,' said Justine kindly, 'but it is none of your fault as to what befell Annabel. We have to put it behind us as Kieran has done. It was an unfortunate accident but we are to thank God she has been found, haven't we,' she said with a matter of fact manner.

As we arrived at Mrs Harding's I had butterflies in my stomach for I did so want to make the right decision. As always Mrs Harding welcomed us into her home and Polly took our bonnets and gloves, after which the dressmaker took us to the room full of bales of materials where I had chosen before.

'I wish to wear white lace,' I blurted out before we began choosing.

'Do you, dear,' said Justine, quite surprised at my words.

'It is most unusual,' said Mrs Harding, 'but I'm sure we can achieve it with a little imagination,' she said kindly, taking us over to one particular table where the white materials were. I looked at all of them not seeing any white lace which I'd set my heart on. 'First of all we need to choose a white silk,' explained Mrs Harding, obviously having seen the crestfallen look on my face. 'For we will need to stitch the lace over it.' At her words I brightened and the butterflies returned.

I chose a plain white silk and then Mrs Harding showed me a bale of lace which was exquisite with intricate motifs of tiny flowers worked on the net, entwined here and there by hearts.

'Yes,' I enthused, 'this is exactly what I had imagined. Now can we talk of what Justine will wear as my bridesmaid, please.'

At my words Justine looked shocked.

'Barbara, I had never thought . . . ' she began.

'I have no-one of my own, Justine, you are the nearest to family I shall ever have. Of course I wish you to attend me at my marriage to your brother,' I told her. 'And can I tell you what I'd like you to wear please?'

'Of course, I am overwhelmed and can hardly believe you have asked me. But what of Kerensa?'

'You know as well as I that Kerensa would not be my bridesmaid even if I asked her, she would utter some unkind retort leaving me wishing I had not mentioned it.'

'Very well,' agreed Justine smiling, 'tell me what you envisage I should wear on your special day.'

So I did.

'I imagine you wearing the white silk and as pink becomes you so a pink cloak draped over the shoulder falling to the upper leg with a white lace bonnet to match the lace of my dress, decorated with small pink roses. How does this sound?' I asked looking at both Justine and the dressmaker.

Arriving back at the castle having being duly measured by both Mrs Harding and Polly, and chattering all the way home about the wedding arrangements Mrs Burnet met us in the hallway.

'I'm really sorry, Miss Justine, but a letter arrived for you yesterday afternoon and what with all the excitement I forgot about it, I'm truly sorry,' The housekeeper apologised handing Justine the letter from the silver salver.

'Thank you, Mrs Burnet. Could you please bring us a tray of tea in the drawing-room?' said Justine accepting the letter from her.

We both walked into the drawing-room removing our bonnets and then sinking thankfully on to the settle by the fire.

'I'll just open my letter while you sit quietly for you must be exhausted by the events of the last twenty-four hours,' said Justine looking down at the envelope in her hands.

I leant back on the settle relaxing when Justine suddenly sat bolt upright on her seat. I looked at her and noted that her hand trembled and her lovely face was ashen in colour.

'Whatever ails you?' I asked her with some concern.

'I'm sorry Barbara, I need to go to my room,' she said rising from the settle.

'Is it bad news?' I called after her as she left the room, but she did not answer me and I never saw her again that day. Mrs Burnet told me after dinner that Miss Justine had taken to her room and wished to be left alone.

That night I felt exhausted yet had less chance of sleep than the night before, which surprised me somewhat as I had had a pleasant day. I lay beneath the sheets imagining what my wedding gown would be like. I knew that Mrs Harding was an excellent dressmaker and would make me an exquisite gown for my marriage.

I was just about to fall asleep when the sobbing started, I sat up in bed but it persisted, so getting up I slipped my robe around me and put some slippers on my feet intent on solving the mystery and praying that this time I wouldn't encounter Derrick in the corridor.

No-one was around so as swiftly as I could I sped along the maze of corridors to Annabel's room, I stood at the door for some time, the sobbing was indeed coming from within the room.

Placing my hand gently on the

doorknob and as quietly as I could turning it, I pushed the door so that I could see around it.

The room was dark, the fire burning low in the grate giving little light, the sobbing was louder yet quieter than I expected it to be.

As my eyes adjusted to the darkness I could see a figure huddled on the armchair by the chimney breast. The sobbing ceased and the woman looked up.

'Who's there?' she called quietly and to my astonishment I could see it was Justine.

9

Justine!' I exclaimed. 'It's you! What on earth is going on? I can't believe you're in here!'

'Yes, it's me, Barbara,' she said quietly, sobs still escaping her lips.

'What is the matter, why do you weep so?' I asked her gently, going over to put my arm around her shoulder.

'It's my mother, sometimes I just can't help feeling so sad about her, and now I've received this letter,' she said, showing me the missive which she was clutching in her hand. 'After twenty years I don't know if someone is playing a joke on me.'

'What does it say, this letter?' I asked with curiosity.

'Read it for yourself. I cannot believe that anyone would play such a cruel trick on me,' she said more rationally now, her sobs subsiding as she handed me the letter. I opened it up, smoothing it out for it had crumpled somewhat in Justine's hand and looking at it with some difficulty by the dim light from the fire I read,

Shrewsbury the 26th February, 1842.

Dear daughter,
You will be shocked and surprised to hear from your mother after twenty years, for I left Rowan Castle when you were only eight years of age. I have been living in Venice where I have pursued my love of painting and am back in Shrewsbury to visit a sick friend.
What your father has told you, if anything, before his death, of my leaving I have little idea. Although this will be a shock to you, could you see it in your heart to come and see me. I would come to Rowan, but I don't somehow think that I would be made welcome. I am staying in room 44 at the Duchess Hotel and will be

here until the 7th of March.

I wish to explain to you what happened all those years ago and would find it easier to tell my daughter than my sons. You can send a message to me here at any time and I pray you will see it in your heart to do so.

Your mother,
Annabel Alexander.

I read the letter through twice before looking at Justine.

'I think this is a genuine letter and you must go to her. I would were I in your position,' I told her honestly.

'Do you really think so?' she said, taking the letter from my hand and reading through it once more. 'You are right, Barbara. I must go and see her, for there is much I wish to know. Please say you will accompany me,' she pleaded.

'I will come with you, for I can see that you need some company,' I said thoughtfully.

'Thank you, Barbara. We can tell

Kieran and Derrick that we are going to pick a headdress and shoes, which indeed we can,' Justine said brightly, for now she had a purpose and I wished to help her for this sadness could not continue.

'This is your mother's room, isn't it?' I asked.

'Yes it is, and for many years I did not bother with it, but for the past few months I have felt that life is passing me by and I kept wondering if I had a mother, would things have been different and a great sadness came over me. That's when I decided to busy myself and create mother's room just as I remembered it. On the days I feel the sadness I come here and somehow it helps me, I have cried so many tears in this room,' Justine told me.

'I know, for since I have been in the yellow room I have heard you,' I told her. 'But no more, we will visit your mother and hopefully you can put all this sadness behind you,' I encouraged her. 'Now, let us go back to bed for it is chilly in here now the fire has burned low and also very dark.' At which words we giggled, and made our way back to our rooms linking arms.

So it was that two days later Justine and I were in the carriage travelling to Shrewsbury, our trunks along with us. Kieran had been delighted for us to go without any suspicion and as we drew away from the steps at Rowan Castle, my betrothed stood by the door waving to us until we were out of sight.

Justine and I had needlework to keep us busy through the evenings, for I was needing petticoats and nightdresses. We were becoming closer as each day went by for which I was thankful, for I was growing ever fonder of her.

We arrived at the Duchess Hotel in Shrewsbury at nearly four o'clock in the afternoon, it was a very grand place which overlooked the River Severn. We swept into the lobby, Justine in the pink which so became her and me in my royal blue outfit which I had worn to the hearing which now seemed such a long time ago.

We were to share an apartment and as Justine signed the register I looked around me at the round marble pillars and all the activity which was going on in the foyer. Through french windows I could see tables laid for dinner with white and yellow tablecloths, the glasses shining even from here. How things had changed for me, I mused, in such a short space of time.

We chose to walk up the wide sweeping staircase, the gold-coloured carpet thick and soft beneath our feet. The doors along the corridor were white and gold with gold inlaid in the cream wallpaper.

How luxurious it all seemed to me and when I saw our apartment my breath was almost taken away; gold brocade covered the couch which was drawn up before a white marble fireplace which was inlaid with gold and the luxurious gold carpet continued in here also, while two beds with white and gold bed heads stood in each alcove, a gold quilt carefully covering the mattresses.

A fire burned in the beautiful grate emitting a warmth for which I was thankful for after the long journey, I felt decidedly cold.

'There's a bathroom!' exclaimed Justine as she opened a door. I went across to look at what she'd discovered. We stood side by side inside the doorway gazing at the huge white enamel bath with large gold taps which stood in the middle of an otherwise almost empty room, apart from a very grand washbasin decorated with pink roses and green leaves. Justine and I hugged each other.

'What an adventure!' I said going across to the ottoman which stood at the end of one of the beds and laying my bonnet on it.

'Come and look at the view,' said Justine who was standing by the window. The light was now fading outside, but I could see the river, the lamplight reflecting an orange glow on the water. There were still people arriving and we stood for some time watching the comings and goings.

'I think we should freshen up and leave a message for your mother at the desk,' I said to Justine. 'And then maybe we should have dinner and an early night.'

To which Justine agreed, just as there was a discreet knock at the door, and on opening it, I could see that our luggage had been brought up by two porters in very grand gold silk waist-coats. They put our trunks where I'd indicated and I reached in my reticule for two florins to give the young men as Kieran had instructed me.

After washing away the grime of the journey and changing into evening gowns, Justine in blue, which matched her piercing blue eyes and I in a soft green which brought Kerensa to mind. We'd not seen her since she had put a curse on Kieran and I that fateful day; at the thought of him I suddenly felt homesick for Rowan Castle.

We walked down the staircase and young men lifted their hats to us, stopping to let us pass. We nodded in acknowledgement and one particular young man with dark hair and warm brown eyes smiled at Justine and bowed before her. As we reached the lobby, Justine looked back to see him retracing his steps down the stairs.

'Can I escort you to dinner, ladies?' he asked in a cultured voice. He was tall and prepossessing and Justine had obviously warmed to him.

'We have to leave a message for someone,' she said and looked at me.

'We'd be delighted for you to accompany us, Sir,' I said, 'if you will excuse us for a moment.'

The young man hovered behind us at a discreet distance and I could see as I observed him that he didn't take his eyes off Justine. We left a message for Mrs Annabel Alexander in room 44 to join us for coffee in the foyer tomorrow morning at eleven.

Our business attended to, the young man took each of us by the arm and escorted us into the dining-room. We sat at a round table with gleaming wine glasses and sparkling cutlery laid on a white damask tablecloth. While I was taken with my surroundings, Justine was taken with the young stranger.

'It is rude,' he began, 'to ask a lady's name before offering one's own. I am Daniel Madison from Wales and I feel the most fortunate of men to have encountered two such lovely young ladies,' he said, all the while looking at Kieran's sister.

The evening went well, we found that he was on business in Shrewsbury and lived in Porthmadog which was quite close to Rowan Castle.

Justine laughed and chatted all evening, her mother quite forgotten, for which I was pleased. I had not seen her so animated and alive since I had met her. We left Mr Madison at the foot of the staircase, agreeing to walk with him by the river after breakfast the next morning.

On reaching our room, Justine couldn't stop talking about him and I was pleased for her and prayed that the association would fair well. Which it did, with me walking a few steps behind them the following morning as we walked alongside the lovely river; which brought to mind my walks with Kieran, and then it was time to meet Annabel.

We sat together anxiously on a gold couch in the foyer looking at every middle-aged woman who walked past us; and suddenly, there she was standing before us in a cream-coloured gown. I recognised her instantly from the portrait and so did Justine, age had not altered Annabel Alexander much, except for a few streaks of grey hair she looked as she had when she had come to Rowan as a bride.

'Mother?' questioned Justine as she stood up and went towards the lovely woman and they embraced each other so suddenly that tears sprang to my eyes. When they had drawn apart, mother and daughter sat together and I felt intrusive.

'Would you like me to leave you?' I asked.

'Who is your charming friend?' asked Annabel, her voice soft with a trace of the Welsh accent still in her speech.

'This is Barbara, who will shortly be my sister-in-law,' Justine introduced me. 'And I would like you to stay, if that is all right with you, Mother?' she said and I noticed there was no hesitation when she spoke the word 'Mother'. And as they talked while we drank coffee from delicate white china cups, it was as if the years between them meeting again had dropped away.

'So you are to marry my son?' said Annabel gently, including me in the conversation.

'Yes, I truly am most fortunate,' I told her honestly.

'How I wish I could be there to see it,' she said wistfully.

'Well you can, Mother. Please return from Venice to attend Kieran and Barbara's wedding,' pleaded Justine.

'But it is not as simple as that,' said

Annabel laying a hand gently on Justine's arm, 'your two brothers may not wish me to come to Rowan. They may not be so welcoming as you and I couldn't blame them.'

'Why did you leave?' asked Justine, 'For you said in your letter you wished to explain. Whatever the reason I am so pleased to have you here and would like nothing more than for you to come to Rowan and sleep once more in your room.'

'I would like that too, now your father is gone,' Annabel said, looking directly into Justine's eyes. 'I will tell you simply why I left you all as young children. Your father beat me many times until I was black and blue when he was drunk; and then he brought his mistress to the castle. How I hated him for that, she had red hair and beautiful green eyes and he paraded her in front of me.

'The beatings I could stand for all your sakes, but not the humiliation of having Hannah strutting around the castle as if it were her own. So I left one dark night with little to my name except the clothes I stood up in and a valise containing miniatures of my children and a few personal belongings.

'I loved to paint and fled to Venice where I painted day and night to try and mend a broken heart, for my heart ached for the three of you, but there could be no return, and thank God Jacob never found me or he would have dragged me back by my hair.' Here she stopped.

'And why have you not contacted us before?' While Justine asked the question, I thought of the red-haired Hannah and Kerensa, the similarity was surely more than a coincidence.

'Because, my child, I didn't know how you would receive me. This is the first time in twenty years that I have stepped on English soil and I knew this may be the only chance I get to make amends,' she told her daughter. 'I heard of Jacob's death, but feared to come too soon.'

'How I wish you had, Mother,' said Justine with tears in her eyes.

'Hannah I know had a child and Hannah herself died not long after the child was born,' said Annabel.

'It must be Kerensa,' Justine said more to herself than to us. 'I've always hated her and now I hate her even more,' she said vehemently.

'You mustn't blame her,' said Annabel softly.

'But I do,' said Justine, 'for she is rude and arrogant.'

'Her mother's daughter then,' observed Annabel.

'I had my suspicions that she may be our father's child for he left a clause in his will that she should not marry my brothers, so it doesn't come as a shock. What I want now more than anything, is for you to come to Rowan for Barbara's wedding,' Justine pleaded once more. 'We will go back and speak to Kieran and Derrick to pave the way for you. Please say you will come.'

'What I will do is delay my return to

Venice. When you arrive home you can send word to me and if all is well I will visit Rowan and then make a decision about the wedding, which is when?' she said, looking kindly at me.

'August the twenty-eighth,' I told her. 'We are to look for my wedding shoes while we are in Shrewsbury, if you'd care to join us.'

'I'd be delighted,' she replied, clapping her hands together and I thought how I'd taken to this gentle woman who was indeed the mother of my betrothed. We talked of Rowan and told Annabel when she asked that Mrs Burnet was still housekeeper.

'Peggy Burnet is a treasure, I will be so pleased to see her and her husband, David, again. But my sons, they are the most important thing at Rowan, along with yourself, Justine.' As we were talking, Daniel Madison walked across the foyer, he stopped in front of us.

'Good morning, ladies. I wish you a pleasant day,' he said with a smile on his face.

'Please join us for dinner this evening. I'm sure my mother won't mind,' said Justine, looking at Annabel.

'If it pleases you, then it pleases me,' Annabel said with a gleam in her eye and I knew that she'd guessed, as I had that her daughter was falling for this young man.

We spent the afternoon in the opulent lounge and for a while I left them to talk of the past. I was more than relieved that things had gone so well between them. I just prayed that Kieran and Derrick would take to it kindly as well.

I guessed that Kieran would be greatly pleased to see her, but I had been unable so far to fathom Derrick out and since the incident in the dim corridor that night, I had kept my distance from him as much as possible.

We dined that evening in the gleaming dining-room with Annabel and Mr Madison. Justine looked radiant in a peach-coloured gown, the off-the-shoulder style complimented her lovely cream skin. Annabel wore a gold-coloured gown inset at the neck with lace which caused to remind me of my wedding gown. Annabel was every inch a lady and although I had never known her husband, Jacob, I hated him for what he had put this beautiful lady through.

My heart bled for her that she was obliged to leave her children because of a monster of a man, which undoubtedly he had been.

Staying in Shrewsbury two more days, we walked and dined with Justine's mother and the charming Daniel Madison. By the time our last morning had arrived Justine confessed that she was in love with him.

'Please will you allow me to ask him to your wedding, for if I don't see him again I will die!' she said, and how could I refuse such an urgent request. I was so happy for her.

We had spent a happy afternoon at a department store, I'd chosen petticoats, nightdresses and undergarments as there had been no time to spend sewing as we had planned.

'Look at this,' said Justine as we passed briefly through the men's department. I looked at what she'd spotted. It was a man's embroidered waistcoat, the white flowers embroidered on grey silk was perfect and with much frivolity, I purchased it for Kieran.

The time came for us to leave, Justine was practically distraught at leaving her mother for fear she may not see her again, but I encouraged her saying that all would be well, which I prayed it was. It had been a most fruitful journey. Justine had found her mother and an attentive beau who had agreed to attend our wedding.

As we sat in the carriage, our parcels around us, I was elated and so looking forward to seeing Kieran and Rowan, I could not have known what menace was to befall me before my wedding day.

10

Justine and I arrived back at Rowan Castle, exhausted. We chatted all the way back about Annabel and Daniel Madison. Kieran's sister seemed like a different person from the one who had left Rowan Castle three days ago, and I was so pleased to think there would be no more sleepless nights spent sobbing in Annabel's room.

Kieran came across to greet us as we stepped into the hallway. 'Sister, Barbara,' he began. 'I trust it was a good journey and that you fared well,' he said, looking at the parcels which were being brought into the hall by David.

'We have had a splendid time, haven't we, Barbara?' enthused Justine. 'But we are tired,' she said, laughing, and I knew that Kieran must see a difference in his sister's manner and it was to turn out that he had, for he said to me when we were alone later.

'Justine seems happy. What manna from heaven has fallen to make her such?' he asked with some amusement.

We sat on the two settles in the drawing room and I thought back to the Duchess Hotel. Justine and I had agreed for me to tell Kieran about Mr Madison, but I was to wait for Justine to tell her brother about their mother.

'She has met a beau,' I told Kieran simply.

'Has she indeed. I never imagined that my sister would fall in love, but I guess she has?' he asked me.

'It would seem she has, Sir. He is a nice young man who lives not far away and we have invited him to our wedding,' I told him.

'Have you indeed,' Kieran replied light-heartedly. 'Well, I shall look forward to meeting this fellow, whoever he may be.' As he spoke, Justine entered the room.

'I have something to tell you also,' she said awkwardly.

'Then I shall go and organise some coffee while you talk to each other,' I said tactfully, noticing Justine held the letter in her hand.

As I made my way across the hall to the kitchens, Kerensa stopped me. 'So you are back. My prayers have not been answered then,' was all she said before making her way up the staircase.

Later that evening while I was showing Megan the purchases I had made in Shrewsbury, Justine came in to tell me that all had gone well with Kieran as I suspected it might, for I knew that Kieran loved his mother as much as Justine.

'And I am to send word to her to come and join us for a few days,' said Justine excitedly. Megan had listened without conscious thought to our conversation.

'Is the first mistress coming back?' she asked wide-eyed. 'Mrs Burnet will be well pleased as she always speaks of her with affection.' At her words, I told Megan not to mention it to anyone, far better I thought that Justine and her siblings told the household staff in their own way.

A few days later I made the decision to visit the waterfall while Kieran was on estate business. I was asking Mrs Burnet who could accompany me when Kerensa crossed the hall.

'I will go with you,' she said sweetly, and I accepted her offer with little thought to the consequences, except to think momentarily that the lovely young woman had stated that she hated Rowan Falls.

So we set off in the pony and trap which Kerensa steered like someone possessed. Thankfully we came safely to a halt where Kieran and I had stopped on my first visit. As we stepped down from the trap, I heard a rumble of thunder in the distance and could see that the skies were rapidly darkening.

'Maybe we should return,' I said.

'The storm is far away for the moment,' Kerensa replied just as I saw a flash of lightning in the distance and another rumble of thunder came ever nearer than before. I suddenly felt afraid and was hesitant about walking to the waterfall, but Kerensa had already started walking.

As I looked at her going on ahead of me, I thought how she was not dressed for this visit at all. Her blue silk dress with a cloak to match moved as one with her. Everything about her was beautiful, from the way she walked to her perfect features. I followed on in my heavy cornflower blue dress, pulling my shawl tighter around me as I followed her, for the sun had disappeared and I felt cold.

The falls still thundered on their way down the gorge, and the water frothed on to the boulders below, hissing like a cauldron. A few drops of rain started to fall and above the roar of the water I heard another clap of thunder. I caught hold of Kerensa's arm as she looked at the swirling mass of water below and then I stepped back, feeling suddenly dizzy just as the rain started to fall heavier and lightning lit the skies above us.

Kerensa had not heard my plea to return above the thundering sound of the water, and then suddenly without warning, she caught hold of my arm, pushing me to my knees and all I could see were the huge boulders below with the water angrily raging over them.

I managed to get to my feet, but stumbled and fell to my knees once more, with Kerensa holding tightly to my arm. She screamed some words in my ear.

'You must go like Annabel, for he is mine!' I looked up at her, her face ugly with hatred. Our clothes were getting damp and I shivered more from fright than cold as the thunderstorm raged above us and the rain now fell heavier.

I struggled to rise to my feet but she was strong and was pushing my face ever nearer the edge. Then without warning she dragged me to my feet. I could not fight her for I felt weak and we were both drenched from the rain, our clothes and hair sodden with water.

I looked at her for a brief moment, there was no beauty or pity there now, I knew that her intent was to push me to my death below. Silently I prayed and thought of Kieran. It all happened in seconds, but suddenly Kerensa was pulled from me and to my relief I could see Kieran's handsome face and as he gathered me in his arms I fell into unconsciousness.

When I awoke again I could see that I was in the master bedroom lying between crisp white sheets, candlelight flickered on the walls as did the firelight and I could make out a figure sitting by the bed, it was Mrs Burnet.

'Thank you, Lord,' she said, more to herself than to me, 'I'll fetch the master and a nice hot mug of sweetened milk for you, Miss.'

I couldn't speak for I felt weak and the horror of what had happened to me came to mind and although I was warm and safe I shuddered at the thought of how I so nearly came to my end as poor

Annabel had done.

Kieran arrived with Justine not many minutes later. They told me Kerensa had been told the circumstances of her birth and had sadly become deranged, they had taken her to stay with their governess, Miss Hewitt for the time being, a kindly lady who had known the four of them from childhood, with the hope that in time her condition would improve.

I had agreed with some reluctance not to bring charges against her. I couldn't say that I was sorry she had gone from Rowan. Not only had she tried to murder me by daring to try and push me in the swollen river, but she had been unkind since my arrival at Rowan Castle.

Although at the same time feeling some pity for her, for it must be hard to love someone as Kerensa loved Kieran and see them with someone else, causing the object of your affection to appear out of reach. But Kerensa knew now that she was Kieran's half-sister and hopefully would in time let it go.

Kieran came to see me every few hours, as did his mother, Annabel, who had arrived back at Rowan. As Kieran and his mother sat by my bed, I was delighted to see how well they were getting on. My betrothed looked somehow different with his mother at his side.

They were both relaxed and happy, and on one occasion Kieran took hold of my hand, 'We had buried Annabel,' he told me gently, 'I am pleased really that you were indisposed.'

'I would have coped with it,' I answered, 'for she has done me no harm.'

'The fact remains that I should not have considered marrying you so soon. Please say you forgive me,' he pleaded in earnest.

'I forgive you your folly,' I assured him, 'and I am pleased Annabel is finally at rest.'

'Thank you, dear heart,' Kieran replied

lifting my hand to his lips, 'I truly love you.'

'And I you,' I told him softly.

I got stronger and one day felt able to share a family celebration for the first Annabel's return to Rowan, which gave me the chance to wear my lovely turquoise gown. As I stepped into the drawing room, the silk moving with me I had eyes for no-one but my betrothed and he for me.

Derrick had been quite amenable about his mother's return, but being the youngest he barely remembered Annabel so didn't have the love for her that Kieran and Justine had. Everything seemed to be falling into place nicely. We spent a lovely summer at Rowan, Justine and Daniel became engaged in July.

Kieran and I spent many hours sat on a bench in the rose garden, the heady scent of the blooms surrounding us. We talked of many things, the second Annabel included, and a few days before our wedding we walked to her grave and laid a single white rose on the soft mound of earth. Neither of us spoke, but we both knew Annabel's death had been a tragic accident and Kieran genuinely repented for the error of his ways.

A week before our wedding date, Justine and I visited Mrs Harding to be fitted for our gowns. We both sat in Mrs Harding's fitting room full of anticipation while the dressmaker and Polly fetched the gowns.

'Here you are, Miss,' said Mrs Harding as she returned. I looked at the white silk and lace creation which she held over her arms and could have burst into tears.

After removing my pale yellow gown and standing in my petticoats Polly slipped the gown over my head, it fell shimmering to the floor. While Polly did up the hooks and eyes I thought once more how lucky I was, indeed, lucky to be alive I mused.

Looking in the mirror at my reflection I thought back to the grim day I had first wed Kieran in my poplin skirts, now looking at myself, this dress was all I had ever imagined.

'Thank you so much!' I said to the dressmaker and Polly, wishing to hug them both, but knowing it would not be seemly to do so.

The twenty-eighth of August arrived and the sun shone in a clear blue sky, the boughs of the trees were laden with leaves and everything looked so different to the snow-covered scene I had witnessed on my arrival at Rowan Castle.

Megan proudly helped me prepare for my wedding, she did my hair in a knot at the back of my head which the orange blossom headdress fitted over perfectly and deftly Megan fixed my veil to it, drawing the front of the veil over my face.

Annabel had brought me a spray of orange blossom and lily-of-the-valley to carry, my wedding slippers fitted perfectly and at last I was ready. Derrick was to accompany me down the aisle, he looked handsome in his black frock coat and as the doors of the chapel were opened for us he said, 'You look beautiful, would that I were the bridegroom.' And he squeezed my hand smiling at me and I realised at that moment that he was, indeed, harmless enough.

I had a fleeting thought of Kerensa as Derrick and I stood together waiting to walk down the aisle. I'd learnt from Kieran that Hannah Templeton had left her daughter a vast fortune, and I hoped that one day in the future it would help Kerensa get her life on the right path. But today was for Kieran and I, whatever else happened, we had both agreed to put the bad things behind us.

In the congregation I could see Peggy Burnet, her David and the household staff dressed in their Sunday best. Annabel Alexander stood proudly by her son with Daniel Madison next to her, who looked back at Justine as she walked behind us dressed in pink and white. And then I saw Clarissa's face smiling at me. Dear Clarissa, my joy was now complete, and I knew this must have been Kieran's doing.

The sun streamed through the stained-glass window spilling a multi-coloured light on the floor before us, and as we walked, my handsome bridegroom wearing the embroidered waistcoat I'd brought him, smiled at me watching my progress towards him and I felt serene and happy at last. The skirts of my lovely dress brushing the floor with each step, at last it was as I'd dreamt, love, happiness and white lace.

THE END

We do hope that you have enjoyed reading this large print book.

Did you know that all of our titles are available for purchase?

We publish a wide range of high quality large print books including:
**Romances, Mysteries, Classics
General Fiction
Non Fiction and Westerns**

Special interest titles available in large print are:
**The Little Oxford Dictionary
Music Book, Song Book
Hymn Book, Service Book**

Also available from us courtesy of Oxford University Press:
**Young Readers' Dictionary
(large print edition)
Young Readers' Thesaurus
(large print edition)**

For further information or a free brochure, please contact us at:
**Ulverscroft Large Print Books Ltd.,
The Green, Bradgate Road, Anstey,
Leicester, LE7 7FU, England.
Tel:** (00 44) **0116 236 4325
Fax:** (00 44) **0116 234 0205**

Other titles in the
Linford Romance Library:

IN A WELSH VALLEY

Catriona McCuaig

When Ruth Greene's cousin Dora has to go into hospital, Ruth's family rallies round by going to look after the grocery shop she runs in her Welsh mining village in Carmarthenshire. This gives them a respite from the London blitz, but other dangers and excitements await them in their temporary home. Young Basil gets into mischief, while their daughter, Marina, falls in love for the first time. But can her wartime love endure?